SWORD OF DAMOCLES

After reports of strange occurrences are received from London, Paris and New York, Neil Vaughan is called to investigate. Gold, uranium and other precious metals are vanishing before the eyes of the men on guard. Vaughan is soon convinced that no human can be responsible, and that it's the work of some sinister outside force. And when Neil and his colleague Ann Delmar are abducted, they become entangled in a terrifying conspiracy that threatens to destroy the world.

SYDNEY J. BOUNDS

SWORD OF DAMOCLES

Complete and Unabridged

LINFORD
Leicester

First published in Great Britain

First Linford Edition
published 2008

British Library CIP Data

Bounds, Sydney J.
    Sword of Damocles.—Large print ed.—
Linford mystery library
    1. Extraterrestrial beings—Fiction
    2. Detective and mystery stories
    3. Large type books
    I. Title
    823.9′14 [F]

    ISBN 978–1–84782–111–9

Published by
F. A. Thorpe (Publishing)
Anstey, Leicestershire

Set by Words & Graphics Ltd.
Anstey, Leicestershire
Printed and bound in Great Britain by
T. J. International Ltd., Padstow, Cornwall

This book is printed on acid-free paper

Prologue

The trouble was presaged by an un-precedented crop of strange reports to the columns of the world's newspapers — reports that heralded the catastrophe about to overtake modern civilization.

Yet nothing was done and no one showed an inkling of suspicion about what might lie behind the reports. To say that they were ignored is an understate-ment; they were laughed at — and never was ridicule more costly. It was not as if the reports were confined to one locality; they came from all quarters of the globe, from Stockholm to Valparaiso, from Istanbul to Bruges, from the Celebes to Fort Yukon.

To quote examples:

From the *London Daily News* for October 9th. 'A procession of orange and green lights was observed travelling across the night sky over Hastings, Sussex, heading inland. The phenomenon lasted only a few minutes.'

From the *Toledo Mercury*, Ohio, U.S. 'What appears to have been a ball of fire shot across the sky above Lake Erie, steering an erratic course. Observers say it was moving at great speed.'

From the *Record*, published in Otago, New Zealand. 'On the night of October 12th, a luminous object was seen to move across the sky, at high speed, and pursuing a parabolic course. No official explanation has so far been given.'

No fewer than one hundred and seventeen separate and similar reports were printed in the space of two months. Presumably a few intelligent men and women noted these reports, and wondered; but what they thought we shall never know, for any conclusions they may have come to were not published in the press

On the other hand, there are plenty of official replies to questions from the public on which we can draw.

'The Ministry has no knowledge of such phenomena.'

'The observations have not been verified.'

'The R.A.F. state that no experimental plane of the type reported has been flown during the past few weeks.'

So much for officialdom; what of the popular press? The articles printed are legion, and we need take only one to show the trend of thought.

From the *Saturday Herald*, a weekend review with a circulation of two-and-a-half million, under the byline of Professor Otto Brunn:

FLYING SAUCERS — THE TRUTH

'So many conflicting reports! What is happening in our night skies? Are there really such things as 'flying saucers'? Let us consider the evidence . . .

'A gigantic wheel with spokes radiating from a central hub is seen floating over the Atlantic; rays of light flash out from it.

'A rotating disc, apparently no thicker than a sheet of ordinary steel plate, surmounted by a turret — and lights dotted round the rim.

'Three circular objects flying in vee formation, luminous and travelling fast . . . '

And so on, for six columns, concluding:

'The credulity of the human race is staggering. There is no evidence whatever to support a theory of 'flying saucers' and it remains only to state the true nature of the objects seen in the sky — nothing more exciting than ordinary *meteorological balloons*!'

The credulity of Professor Brunn is equally staggering; perhaps he never observed the phenomena himself, but other scientists did.

'At one-forty a.m. on October the sixteenth,' wrote Doctor Philip Steer of the Dulwich Observatory in an official report, 'I was studying the night sky through my telescope. I saw a cigar-shaped object with a red trail emanating from it, moving very fast from south to north. It remained in view for one-and-one-half minutes, and until cloud obscured my view, was sharply defined and clearly in focus.'

Strange behaviour indeed for a meteorological balloon! Doctor Steer contented himself with the bare observation, assigning no cause. It would seem that the scientific world was a little afraid of what it might find by probing too deeply into the unknown.

So much for surface indications of what was to follow . . . other events, not made public, were occurring about the same time — events which alarmed the heads of government throughout the world. In France, in the United States, and in Britain, dramatic scenes were being enacted.

At the White House in Washington, the President was quartered with the Secretary of State and the head of the Atomic Commission.

'There can be no mistake?' asked the President.

'None,' came the prompt answer. 'Over the last few weeks a substantial quantity of uranium 235 has disappeared from our secret stockpiles. Full security precautions have been taken, yet the leakage continues. It would seem physically impossible for the metal to be removed, but — still the uranium vanishes.'

The Secretary's lips curled.

'Perhaps you will take heed of my warnings now, Mr. President? For years I have preached against the re-emergence of the red menace, only to be fobbed off with the puerile platitudes of those who place lip service to democracy before national security. Obviously those responsible for this threat to our atomic stockpiles are spies and traitors in the pay of Moscow. The Russians — '

'You've got Communism on the brain,' snorted the head of the Atomic Commission. 'The Russians are, after all, only human — and no human agency can spirit away uranium 235 without leaving some trace.'

The President gestured helplessly.

'Then what is the answer?'

He received no answer, for no one knew.

At Paris, in the Chamber of Deputies, a select body of ministers was debating a similar issue; while at No. 10 Downing Street, the Prime Minister had called the cabinet to secret session.

'The matter is serious,' said the P.M. 'It seems incredible that so large a quantity of uranium should disappear as if into thin air. Something must be done, and immediately.'

A long silence indicated that those seated round the table had no idea what must be done. Then the Minister of War cleared his throat.

'Security must be increased, of course, and the military guards doubled. However, in view of the particular nature of the loss, I suggest it is more a matter for another department. Surely some scientific means can be employed to detect the movement of this metal?'

Another Minister answered.

'Scientific devices are used every day to check the distribution of uranium 235. It is impossible for any radioactive material to be moved without the knowledge of our scientists — yet the impossible happens!'

The P.M. looked unhappy.

'What information we have,' he said, 'points in one direction only — that some responsible person at the plant is behind this theft. No one else could possibly make away with it.'

'A full investigation will be held?'

'This must be kept secret,' interposed the Minister of War sharply. 'If news of this leaked out — ' He paused. 'I trust everyone understands that this heavy loss of uranium means that our projected programme of nuclear re-armament will be held up? In the event of war, the initiative will be with the enemy.'

The P.M. rapped the table for silence.

He said: 'I have decided that this affair calls for unusual measures and, therefore, I propose to place the matter in the hands of one man — a man you know well, for he has served us on previous occasions. Neil Vaughan.'

'Too young,' someone objected. 'A more experienced man . . . '

'It is partly because he is young that I have decided on him — an older man would be inclined to follow routine. And the mysterious circumstances that sur-round the loss of our uranium definitely call for a fresh mind, someone not afraid to break with tradition and follow his own nose. Besides which, he has special qualifications for the job, having studied the physical sciences before joining M.I.5.'

No one else objected: no one else had

an alternative to offer. The meeting broke up, the faces of the Ministers showing alarm mingled with relief; alarm lest the disappearance of uranium should not be stopped — relief at passing the responsibility to someone else . . . Neil Vaughan.

1

Top Secret

The door was at the end of a long passage lit by fluorescent tubes, and the joining of walls and floor was effected by a smooth concave arc of concrete to prevent dust collecting. There were no windows, but the air was fresh, the quiet purring of ventilator motors constantly in the background. The door was marked:

MR. IRWIN

Neil Vaughan knocked and waited. A voice called: 'Come in.'

He went in. The room was large and airy, simply furnished. Across a large, flat-topped table, a man sat in a comfortably padded chair. Irwin rose immediately, came round the table and gripped Vaughan's hand.

'Good to see you, Neil,' he said. 'Sit down.'

Irwin, head of M.I.5, was in his early fifties, a man of military bearing, his hair touched with iron-grey. Perhaps the most conspicuous feature of his appearance was the smallness of his feet; they were very small for the size of his body, encased in pointed, highly-polished black shoes, and gave his movements a mincing quality.

Irwin retreated back round the table and eased himself into his chair. Vaughan sat down too, across the table from him.

Irwin said, 'I've a job for you, something rather special. It is at the Prime Minister's personal recommendation that you are to take charge.'

Vaughan leaned forward in his chair, suddenly interested.

Standing he topped the six foot mark and had the ruggedness of an open-air enthusiast. His face was not over-handsome with strongly marked features, an aquiline nose and deep-set eyes of grey — the jaw line masked by a thick, black beard. His hair, too, was black.

His relaxed air was deceptive for he was slow neither of thought nor movement. At thirty he was still unmarried.

Abruptly Irwin said: 'This is something big. Let me put you in the picture, then you can study these.' He pushed a file of reports across the table. 'You know we have an atomic research plant at Dunstead?' Vaughan nodded. 'Uranium 235 is disappearing in large quantities . . . '

While Irwin was speaking, Vaughan recalled certain facts to mind. 235 was an isotope of natural uranium. It was the basic fuel for an atomic power plant and equally important in the manufacture of atom bombs. Only a small amount could be obtained from a vast quantity of natural uranium — and separation was a costly and intricate procedure. Furthermore, the stuff was dangerous to handle on account of its radioactive properties.

The more he thought about the handling techniques, the elaborate precautions which each step in manufacture entailed, and the security checks, the harder it became for him to credit the substance of Irwin's words. When the head of M.I.5 had finished, he said:

'It sounds impossible. No one could get the stuff out of Dunstead and remain undetected.'

Silently, Irwin pushed the file at him. Vaughan opened the covers and read, carefully, each report. In detail, the papers gave the facts of the loss, covering a period of three weeks. Some were by the research staff, others by the security people. The information covered only the disappearance of uranium — no one had any idea where it had gone, or how.

It was a simple story, yet quite staggering in its implications.

Vaughan repeated: 'It's impossible.'

Irwin nodded slightly.

'Quite. Your job is to find out who is taking the stuff, and how — and where it is going. You have a free hand. Report direct to me and I'll pass word to the P.M. I need not stress that no inkling of this must reach the public.

'I have two passes to admit you to Dunstead,' Irwin went on. 'I imagine you'll start the investigations there.'

'Two?'

'Yes. Your opposite number is flying over from the States. I gather they have similar trouble. As a matter of fact, I am expecting him any minute now.'

Vaughan thought about that, startled. Britain *and* the U.S. losing uranium . . .

'And the other nuclear countries?' he asked softly.

Irwin shrugged.

'Perhaps. Certainly the Russians have been suspiciously quiet of late . . . but how? Anyway, don't worry about that end of it. Our job is to see that no more uranium vanishes into thin air.'

Vaughan made a wry face.

'Sounds simple — but the difficulties of smuggling 235 out of Dunstead must be appalling. Only a large organization could even contemplate it.'

The head of M.I.5 rose from his seat and paced the room, strutting like a bantam cock. He turned on Vaughan abruptly, stopped, and drove one clenched hand into the palm of the other.

'We've got to do something,' he said, 'and fast. If our programme — '

A buzzer interrupted his line of

thought. Irwin pressed down a switch on his desk.

'Yes . . . very well . . . show him up. Oh! I see . . . well, show *her* up.'

Irwin turned to Vaughan with a sour smile.

'The agent from Washington appears to be a member of the opposite sex. I hope you're going to get on well!'

Vaughan made no comment. Both men waited in silence for the girl to arrive, and when the door opened and she came into the room, it was Irwin who moved forward to greet her.

'Welcome, Miss Delmar. May I present Neil Vaughan, who is representing the British Government in this matter?'

Vaughan held out his hand and she touched it briefly.

'Hello, Mr. Vaughan.' She had a southern drawl that was pleasant, on the ear. 'I hope we're going to work well together.'

She had a warm smile and an easy manner.

Vaughan said roughly: 'This isn't the sort of job I'd expect a girl to handle.'

She was not offended. 'My government disagrees with you then. Before I joined Intelligence, I worked on atomic research at a University. I guess you'd say that gives me a kind of edge on this business.'

Vaughan drew up a chair for her and all three sat down. Miss Delmar passed across her papers to Irwin, who checked them through carefully.

Vaughan found himself looking at the girl and deciding she was very easy to look at. Although she was of petite stature, she had a well-shaped figure.

She wore her honey-blonde hair tied back with a ribbon; sat with one leg crossed over the other — seamless nylons and sensible, flat-heeled shoes — and used a perfume which was distinctive without being vulgar. She was, Vaughan thought, about twenty-seven.

Irwin said: 'I understand that America is disturbed over the loss of uranium metal in somewhat mysterious circumstances.'

She laughed lightly.

'Mysterious is right — though impossible would be a better word!'

'We're having the same trouble over here, which is why the Prime Minister has suggested a combined Anglo-American investigation. Results may come quicker that way.' Irwin handed her the file he had given Vaughan to read. 'This is all the information we have to date. It isn't much, I'm afraid.'

Miss Delmar took a pair of folding spectacles from her handbag and adjusted the frame to the contours of her face. They made her look like the screen version of an efficient secretary. She read very fast, turning the pages quickly.

Vaughan kept looking at her, discovering new beauty in her face. The curve of her mouth, subtly accentuated by just the right shade of lipstick; the serious, yet not solemn, expression in her eyes. She was, he thought, going to prove a disturbing element in his bachelor life.

'Just about the same information as I have on our own losses,' she said, putting down the file.

She spoke about the American situation, clearly and incisively, wasting no words but leaving nothing of importance from her statement. Intelligent too, Vaughan noted.

Miss Delmar removed her spectacles, folded them and put them away.

'There's just one thing,' she said, and paused. 'It sounds crazy — but then, the whole affair is. You've seen the reports in the papers, I suppose? You know the sort of thing; moving lights seen in the sky, and stories of 'flying saucers'. Well, I have a hunch there is something behind those reports, that they are connected with the missing uranium.'

Both men looked at her, turning over the idea in their minds.

Irwin said, cautiously: 'You mean, someone is using a new type of aircraft to make away with the stuff?'

'Something like that,' she replied. 'It's just a feeling I have, that the two sets of events are connected. I haven't thought it out, but I'd like to try correlating the times of those things seen in the sky with that of the uranium losses.'

'Newspaper stories are apt to be distorted, if not purely imaginary,' Vaughan said bluntly. 'And even if there is some new aircraft involved, it still does not explain how the uranium is taken from a closely guarded atomic plant.'

'Hmm.' Irwin seemed thoughtful. 'There's probably nothing to it, but it might be an idea to check the times and see if they correspond. I'll put someone on it right away.'

Vaughan stood up.

'The first thing is to go down to Dunstead and look round.' He glanced at the girl. 'You'd like to come along, Miss Delmar?'

'You bet,' the girl said briskly.

Irwin escorted them to the door.

'Keep in touch,' he said. 'I'll ring through to Professor Stanley and advise him you're on your way. Good luck.'

They used a self-operating lift to reach ground level and passed into the court-yard where Vaughan's Daimler was parked.

'Where are you staying?' he asked.

'The *Royal*.'

Vaughan nosed the Daimler into the whirl of London's traffic.

'Right,' he said. 'First stop, the *Royal* — then Dunstead!'

2

Dunstead

They could see the chimneys, two of them, immensely tall, from a long way off. Vaughan kept the Daimler to the centre of the concrete highway, hardly aware of the Autumnal landscape slipping past.

Dunstead was in Surrey, close to the Sussex border, an isolated spot in the heart of the countryside. The hills were wooded, with leafless trees stark against a grey sky, and the hedges and ferns given new life by the reflected glory of fallen leaves, glittering golden-brown after the rain.

It was barely two hours since they had left Irwin. At the *Royal*, Ann Delmar surprised Vaughan by a quick change that had taken only ten minutes; they had eaten a hasty meal and set off directly.

It was she who had insisted that he call

21

her 'Ann' — this was no time to stand on ceremony, she pointed out in her forthright American manner, and began addressing him as 'Neil' right away. Not that Vaughan minded — it gave him a feeling of intimate companionship with this lovely girl who had come so abruptly into his life.

Vaughan slowed the car as a high wire fence came into view, stretching to left and right across the undulating country-side. He stopped at the checkpoint and a security man inspected their passes.

'Keep straight on,' the guard said. 'Security is the first building on the left. Major Johns is expecting you.'

The gate closed behind them and Vaughan drove on. The atomic plant was some miles farther beyond the boundary fence, and the road swung in a long curve, the trees cleared away on either side. In the distance he could see the squat, square buildings of the atomic piles, their four-hundred-foot chimneys soaring skywards. Grouped about the plant, were the workshops and laboratories, storage tanks for waste products, the administration building, powerhouse and medical section.

Vaughan stopped the Daimler outside the security building and he and Ann went inside. Again their credentials were examined; then they were passed to Johns.

The Major was tall and thin, with a sweeping ginger moustache and harassed expression. His face, grey and lined, denoted a very unhappy man.

'Glad you've come, Vaughan,' he jerked out. 'You too, Miss Delmar — perhaps feminine intuition will help here, or the American method. I don't mind telling you that this business has upset me. I'm at a disadvantage not being a scientist — I just can't understand how the stuff is getting out. Naturally, I take the most stringent precautions . . .'

He lapsed into a worried silence, and Vaughan said:

'We'll do all we can to help, Major. Both Miss Delmar and I have some knowledge of atomic physics.'

'Good, good!' Johns brightened at once. 'That's what the job needs, someone who understands the scientific angle. I'm just a plain soldier, and it's quite beyond me. Then there's the professor — Stanley, I mean. Of course, all these boffins are a bit crazy, but I think he's actually glad the uranium has disappeared. Gives him a new problem to solve.'

'Has he learnt anything?' Ann asked quickly.

'No . . . that is, if he has, he hasn't told me. Scientists!' Johns was quite bitter about it. 'I can't follow their lingo, you know. Stanley seems to think there is some scientific explanation for the losses.'

Vaughan's hands were deep in his pockets.

'How many people know about the disappearance of 235?'

'Myself, and my deputy,' Johns replied. 'Stanley, and those directly working in that part of the establishment. Nine all told — which doesn't make the problem any easier. I have the area cordoned off and have taken the necessary steps to see that the rest of the staff learn nothing about it. That's another headache.

Naturally, everybody knows something is in the air, and wants to know what — and I daren't tell them.'

He hesitated, then —

'I suppose you're bound to suspect the few people directly involved, and I can't blame you for that — but it's too fantastic. When you've been here a little while, you'll understand. It's a kind of atmosphere. All the people working on the plant are enthusiasts, completely wrapped up in their jobs — to suspect them of sabotage is out of the question.'

'Right!' Vaughan pulled his hands from his pockets and looked about him, a new briskness in his manner. 'Let's see the professor, then take a look at the plant where the uranium disappeared.'

Major Johns led the way across the broad expanse of concrete to administration. He knocked on a door and walked in.

'Professor Stanley,' he said, 'this is Neil Vaughan from M.I.5, and Miss Delmar of American Intelligence. They both know something about atomic energy, so you won't have to start from the beginning.

They're here to investigate the loss of uranium 235.'

'Ah, yes,' said the professor vaguely, 'an interesting problem, most interesting.' He blinked at them over horn-rimmed spectacles, his gaze wondering. Obviously his mind was on other things. 'I wonder now — ' His voice dropped and he mumbled something to himself, remembered his manners and said: 'Good of you to come. Was there something special you wanted to see me about?'

Johns sighed, and Ann said:

'We've met before, professor, while you were teaching at Cal Tech — I was a student there. I don't suppose you remember me?'

Stanley gave her a little more attention.

'Yes, yes, indeed I do, Miss — er — Miss — ?'

'Delmar.'

'Miss Delmar. Of course, I remember. You were the prettiest student in the class!'

Vaughan grinned; the professor wasn't so dumb. He looked closely at Stanley, studying him. A man in his forties, rather stout, red-faced with a shock of unruly white hair. His vague manner was merely the result of his withdrawn thoughts; he lived inside himself, fully alive in his own field, but only distantly aware of what went on outside. He was dressed in clothes that had been worn long enough to become comfortable; the elbows and knees were baggy.

Vaughan said: 'I should like to tour the plant, professor, starting from the point where the crude ore reaches you, and following through the various processes till we come to the point where the losses occurred. I want you along too, Johns.'

'Certainly, certainly,' the professor agreed. 'It will give me great pleasure to show you round.'

They left the administration block, Stanley walking beside Ann Delmar, and Vaughan following with Johns. They reached the entrance to the plant and, directly inside, were changing rooms separately labelled 'Men' and 'Women.'

Stanley explained: 'All personnel are required to change their clothes before entering an active area, a precaution to prevent radioactive dust from being taken outside.'

Ann left them, and the three men changed into white overalls and caps, rubber boots and gloves. She rejoined them, minutes later, similarly attired. The sight of Vaughan, his bushy black beard projecting like a stage prop above his white suit, made her smile.

'I feel like Snow White,' she whispered in his ear, 'and you must be one of the seven dwarfs!'

At a counter, a clerk issued them with film badges, which they fastened to their overalls.

'A simple device to register the amount of radiation we receive while in the plant,' continued the professor. 'Do not be alarmed, this is purely a precaution as no radiation above the tolerance level is allowed. We are now ready to proceed.'

The first room they entered was stacked high with metal drums.

'This is how we receive the natural ore. When a batch is required, the drums are opened and the ore crushed to powder, then mixed with water to form a slurry for ease of handling — great care must be taken as the dust from uranium is extremely poisonous. Which also explains why there is so little to see; all operations in this department are performed in completely sealed tanks.'

They passed into the next room where white-clad figures were watching meters and adjusting valves.

'The metal uranium is not extracted from the crude ore by smelting,' Professor Stanley stated, 'as with so many metals, but by dissolving it in acid and then treating the solution to extract the part we need. That is what is happening here.'

They moved on again.

'The purified solution is precipitated to form a solid. The metal we have now is uranium 238 and is cast into rods, machined accurately to size and encased in aluminium. Through here — '

He paused at another door, peering through the glass inset.

' — we have the machine shop. As you will see, one operation has just finished and cleaning is in progress, so we will not go inside. Elaborate precautions must be taken at every step, to ensure purity of the finished product. Various tests are made during the canning process, then the cylinders are stored until required.'

Professor Stanley took them across a concrete yard to the storeroom. Inside were steel racks, loaded with aluminium canisters; Johns' men were on guard.

Vaughan asked: 'Nothing missing from here, I suppose?'

'Indeed no,' the professor agreed. 'Only the isotope 235 has been taken.'

Of course, Vaughan thought, natural uranium — that is, 238 — was useless on its own as an atomic fuel.

'How about plutonium, or uranium 233?' Ann put in quickly.

Stanley shook his head.

'Our plutonium stock has not been touched — as for uranium 233, we do not produce that here.'

There was a moment's silence. Vaughan thought hard.

'It amounts to this then,' he said. 'Whoever has removed the uranium is interested only in the naturally-occurring fission material. That is 235. The other two isotopes are artificially created. That seems to me an important point.'

'Agreed,' said the professor, nodding. 'You have summed up the situation accurately.'

They walked on a little way, towards the square concrete buildings housing the two atomic piles. The chimneys were giant cylinders soaring above them.

Vaughan stopped suddenly, pointing to the storage tanks that held waste radioactive products.

'You've checked those, Johns? There hasn't been any switching around?'

'First thing we thought of,' said the security man. 'All waste products have been double-checked. Also the natural uranium and plutonium stores. There is no 235 in the place.'

'Except in the pile that is operating now,' Professor Stanley added.

Vaughan grinned.

'And no one could get at that!'

They entered the first building. It was a vast hall, the centre taken up by the pile itself; in front of that was the control desk, looking rather like a cinema console, with the shift engineer studying meters which relayed information from the interior of the pile.

It was un-dramatic, silent except for the background roar of the blowers pumping cooling air through the plant. There was none of the tension normally found in a powerhouse. Yet it only required a little imagination . . .

Behind thick walls of concrete, the pile was constructed of graphite blocks, channelled to take cylindrical cans of uranium. Control of the reaction was effected by sliding boron-steel rods in and out . . . and the heart of the pile was an atomic furnace equivalent to the sun itself!

'We have two piles, or reactors,' explained Stanley, 'in which the energy of uranium is released in the form of heat. The reaction is started when a neutron hits the nucleus of an atom splitting it in two parts — this is called fission. At the same time, more neutrons are given off, hitting other atoms and again causing fission. This is the well-known chain-reaction.

'This pile is used for changing uranium 238 into plutonium, in other words to create an artificial fission material which can be used as atomic fuel, or in missiles. The second pile — not operating for an obvious reason — is a new type, in which we use 235 to produce power.' Stanley paused, looking about him. 'This pile too must cease to operate before long; as you will realize, we need a small supply of 235 to trigger the reaction.'

They went outside. Between the two piles was a huge water tank.

'The uranium slugs are discharged here, and left to cool,' the professor said.

He led them into the Primary separation plant, a long room fitted with rows of steel tanks.

'Here the irradiated uranium is dissolved in acid and the plutonium separated by a solvent extraction process; the plutonium is further refined before being converted to metal — the end result being a few ounces of fission material for every ton of uranium.'

Outside again, the Professor did not lead them into the second pile. Vaughan knew it would be similar to the first, though not in operation because there was no 235 to fuel it. They moved on to another building.

It was a simple steel framework covered by corrugated sheeting and extending over a large area. Inside, a row of metal cells, each the size of a small house and fitted with instruments, reached down the centre; each cell was controlled by a white-clad operator. It was quiet except for the hum of compressors.

'The gaseous diffusion plant,' commented the professor, 'for separating uranium 235 from 238.'

Johns' ears pricked and he looked round him as if suspecting that the whole trouble could be explained here.

'238 is converted to a gas and pumped through these cells, repeating the process in successive stages on the cascade principle. Uranium 235 is separated in the process — as a gas, of course — and is later changed back to a metal, when it is stored until required.'

They walked through the plant and outside again, to the store sheds. The doors were locked and security men posted. Vaughan thought: After the horse is stolen . . .

They went inside. Thick concrete walls, no windows, and empty steel shelves. Professor Stanley rubbed his gloved hand along one of the benches, as if expecting an invisible barrier to obstruct his motion. There was nothing.

'Uranium 235 was stored here,' he said. 'The doors were always kept locked and a guard posted outside. No metal was removed except on a written order signed by myself. It just . . . disappeared!'

Vaughan went carefully round the room, inspecting walls, floor and roof. The concrete had in no way been tampered with — the door was the only possible exit. And that had been kept locked and guarded.

Johns began to pull nervously on his moustache.

'It's impossible,' he muttered, 'impossible!'

'Quite so,' Vaughan said dryly, 'but it happened.' He turned to Stanley. 'I suppose you've been over the area closely with your instruments? Tell me, can there be any scientific explanation — any at all, no matter how remote?'

The professor appeared lost in thought. Vaughan waited patiently, before asking:

'Surely there would be some radioactivity? *That* can be traced.'

'I know of no possible explanation,' the professor answered, 'but it is an interesting problem. I shall work on it constantly. As for radiation — '

He brought a personal monitor, shaped like a fountain pen, from his pocket, and moved it slowly through a full circle. The quartz fibre did not even tremble.

'Nothing, you see. The uranium has gone, leaving no trace.'

Vaughan looked enquiringly at Ann, but she could suggest nothing.

'All right, Johns,' he said briskly. 'We'll return to your office. I shall want to interrogate all personnel directly concerned in this business, one at a time.'

The security man nodded.

'I expected that, and warned them to stand by.'

They returned to the changing rooms,

stripped off their white uniforms and handed in the film badges for processing. Dressed again in their own clothes, they walked back to Johns' office.

The questioning did not take long. There were seven men involved — and each knew precisely nothing. Vaughan dismissed them and called in Professor Stanley.

'You are preparing another batch of 235, I suppose?'

'Yes,' agreed the professor. 'It should be ready in two or three days.'

'Right! I'm returning to London this evening. I want you to let me know, through Irwin, when the stuff is ready for storing. I'll be coming down to keep an eye on it myself. I think that's all. If you get any ideas, pass them on. If I think of anything, I'll get in touch with you.'

Outside, Ann said: 'Looks like a dead end. What happens now?'

Vaughan could only shrug.

3

Dracula Again!

Bill Clark was night watchman of a warehouse on Bankside, a middle-aged bachelor with ruddy cheeks and starting a paunch. His nerves were good and he kept a large Alsatian dog for company.

He sat in a little office near the main gate of the warehouse, drinking tea and reading an evening paper. His dog lay at his feet, muzzle resting on forepaws and tail stretched out in a straight line. It was two o'clock in the morning.

'Flying saucers,' he said aloud, and snorted. 'The rubbish they print these days!'

The dog opened one eye at the sound of his master's voice, regarded him a moment, then closed his eye again. He moved his tail to show that he was listening.

The newspaper recorded an account by

a pilot who had seen objects in the sky over the south of England.

'The trouble with these pilots is they drink too much alcohol,' Bill Clark said. 'Now me, I stick to a strong cup of tea, and I don't see things in the sky.'

He laughed.

'Of course, I *hear* things, but that isn't the same . . .'

Quite unconsciously he began to listen. The night air was cool and undisturbed by any sound.

'Nothing tonight, at all events,' he grunted. 'Quiet as the grave.'

He remembered other nights, when strange noises had come from the empty building next to the warehouse — very strange noises indeed and unrelated to any natural sound he had ever heard. A kind of scratching and high-pitched squeaking combined, only, well . . . he couldn't imagine the kind of animal that would make such a sound. The first time he'd heard it he got goose pimples.

Reason argued that no kind of sound could come from an empty building anyway. His ears denied this.

He had walked round the warehouse and loading yard, listened at the wall separating him from the building next door.

Nothing happened, and he did not make any report.

The sounds did not come every night. Sometimes they'd miss two or three times in a row; then he'd hear that inhuman scratching and squeaking two nights running. He grew curious, but some inner warning forbade him investigating.

And, tonight, no sound came from the empty building.

'It is empty,' he said aloud, trying to convince himself. 'So I couldn't have heard anything. Imagination, Bill, my boy!'

But curiosity was strong in Bill Clark. He wanted to *know* . . . He'd just pop his head round the door and take a look. After all, whatever had made the noise wasn't there now, or he'd be hearing it again. He rose to his feet.

'Roger!'

The Alsatian obediently followed his master as he picked up a heavy walking stick and electric torch and left the office. Clark moved across the yard under a full moon; beyond the warehouse, the tall masts of ships made a familiar silhouette against the night sky.

Between the two buildings was a high wall and a solitary door; at some time in the past, a previous occupant had rented both buildings, knocked out the brick-work and put in a connecting door. Clark knew all about that, and the rusting bolts on his side of the door; he thought it unlikely there would be similar bolts on the far side.

He put his torch in his pocket and propped the stick against the wall. The bolts were large and hard to move; Clark struggled with them, easing them back in their sockets to an accompaniment of protesting sound. At last both bolts were withdrawn and he tugged at the door. It creaked open and he stood listening at the gap.

The silence remained unbroken.

Clark hesitated. Strictly he had no business to enter this building, but there was a nagging curiosity at the back of his mind. He would just take a quick look round and come out, bolt the door and no one would ever know he had been inside.

He pulled the door wider and flashed his torch through the dark emptiness, taking a step forward. Roger growled deep in his throat and his hair bristled. Clark picked up his stick and took a firm grip on it before proceeding into the building.

He did not need the torch for moonlight streamed down from high, windows, showing a vast empty chamber. The dust on the floor was unmarked. Roger remained at the door, whining.

When Clark called him the dog came reluctantly, slinking at his heels. The night watchman didn't like that — something had made the dog afraid, and he advanced slowly.

There was a peculiar rancid odour that made him wonder what had been stored in the building. He stooped to ruffle Roger's mane, speaking in a soft, crooning voice:

'It's all right, boy — nothing to be

scared of. Just an empty . . . '

His voice faded off as the moonlight flicked out as if a switch had been pulled. Clark stood quite still, his pulse quickening and a jumpy feeling starting in his stomach. Beside him in the darkness, Roger lifted his head and wailed dismally.

No cloud could have passed so swiftly across the face of the moon. Someone, or some thing, had obscured the window.

Clark looked up; and two luminous yellow eyes stared back at him from high in the roof. There came a fluttering, swishing sound — and the high-pitched squeaking he had heard previously.

He was not alone.

His legs shook and fear made his mouth dry. There was something up there, hanging from the rafters. He backed away, stumbled into the dog and lashed out with his stick.

'Shut that damned row!'

Bill Clark fumbled in his pocket for the torch, pointed it at the roof and thumbed the switch. He saw . . . and for a moment, did not understand what he saw. He stared, his eyes recording but his brain

43

making nothing of it at all. A dozen bundles hung from the rafters and small eyes watched him. Bundles? No, *bodies!*

Movement came, a huge black wing shifted, folding and unfolding again — and he saw it was this which had blocked out the moon. Fear paralysed the watchman. That wing — it must be twenty foot across . . . it was impossible!

Some *thing* swooped down from the rafters. He had a glimpse of a furry body, big as a man's, a pointed snout and sharp teeth — then he ran.

Something hit him behind the head and he went down. Memories of a story he had once read raced through his mind. Giant bats . . .

'Dracula again!'

Roger had deserted him, running with his tail between his legs and whining hideously. Clark felt himself lifted through the air. There was blackness, an alien stench; air swished past him and he knew he was falling.

As he hit the concrete there was sudden pain, then nothing any more.

Rubenstein was in his very early twenties. He had a swarthy face and dressed in a quiet lounge suit. He had not long come down from Oxford to be employed at M.I.5, and Irwin had set him to collect data on strange things seen in the sky.

When Vaughan and Ann Delmar joined him on their return from Dunstead, he had compiled a thick dossier of newspaper cuttings.

He looked at them suspiciously, and said: 'This isn't a joke, is it? I've only found one cutting that ties in with the times Mr. Irwin gave me. The first date . . . '

Rubenstein had not been told that the dates referred to the missing uranium at Dunstead.

He read aloud: 'From the *Daily News*. 'Early this morning, a dark shape was reported in the sky over Chichester moving inland at great speed. There was a rush of wind, said to sound like the noise of a waterfall'. That's all. What's it about, Mr. Vaughan?'

Ann interposed: 'Nothing at all on the other dates?'

"Nothing in the newspapers, Miss Delmar. Do you really think there is anything in these reports?'

Vaughan was leafing through the cuttings that Rubenstein had collected, and was staggered by the number of them. Reports from far across the world, from Malaysia, from South America, from islands in the Pacific; reports of lights seen at night, of strange bodies travelling at enormous speeds, of disc-shaped objects flying in formation. The sheer bulk of the material was disturbing.

'Inland from Chichester,' Ann mused. 'That would be the right area, wouldn't it, Neil?' He nodded. 'And without lights — surely that is significant? The noise could indicate that the thing — whatever it is — was lower than usual, perhaps coming down to land.'

For some reason Vaughan felt irritated.

'No sense in jumping to conclusions, Ann. We've no proof there was anything in the sky. And if there was . . . '

He didn't finish. If there had been

46

something . . . the thought was alarming, suggesting unknown powers.

Rubenstein said: 'There are so many of these reports. Can they all be hallucinations?'

Neither Vaughan nor the girl felt like attempting an answer. A new thought struck Vaughan.

'Do you realise,' he said, 'that we are probably the first people to list all the phenomena worldwide? In the ordinary course of events, no one would bother — '

Again, he did not feel like pressing the statement to its logical conclusion.

Ann said, quietly: 'I'll get hold of the relevant dates from my side of the Atlantic, and see if they fit the data.'

Vaughan began: 'It's hardly possible — ' and checked himself. It was hardly possible that uranium 235 could be removed from Dunstead. He turned back to Rubenstein.

'No,' he said, answering their assistant's initial question, 'this isn't a joke. The data you are collecting may not be connected with the job we're working on — then again, it may. We just don't know enough to be sure. But this is one line of enquiry that must be followed through . . . and you can consider it a priority job.'

Rubenstein searched through a batch of cuttings.

'There's one here that — well, read it for yourself!'

Ann took the newspaper clipping and Vaughan read over her shoulder.

From the *New Times*, published in Penang, Malaya. 'An odd story has reached this office from the interior. Apparently, one of the workers on a rubber plantation rushed into his employer's bungalow in a fine state of nerves. According to this man he had seen a huge metal 'thing' in the jungle. It was shaped like a dish, about forty-five feet long, with a dome on top and windows in it. His employer went to the spot and found a depression in the earth as if a great weight had rested there. Of the thing which had caused this depression he saw nothing.'

Rubenstein grinned.

'Sounds to me like the men from Mars have landed!'

4

Data

A telephone bell rang shrilly and insistently. Vaughan groped his way out of a second sleep, fumbled for the receiver on the stand by his bed, and said:

'Hello.'

'Neil? This is Ann. Have you seen this morning's headlines?'

He became alert, sitting up and pushing back the sheets.

'No. What is it?'

'Something very odd happened in a disused building on Bankside. I have a hunch we should investigate.'

Vaughan thought quickly.

'All right. Have you had breakfast yet? No? Well, come round here and I'll feed you, then we'll go on together.' He listened again. 'And Ann — '

'Yes?'

'You have a lovely voice.'

49

She laughed and broke the connection.

He called the porter of his service flat and asked for a newspaper to be sent up, washed and dressed quickly. The paper was delivered and the headlines announced:

DRACULA IN LONDON!

Thereafter followed a lurid account of mysterious happenings in a deserted building on Bankside. A night watchman, Bill Clark, had been found dying after his dog had brought a policeman to the scene by its continual howling. Nothing was definitely known, and the headlines had grown out of Clark's last words before he died . . .

'*Giant bats*,' he had repeated, over and over. '*Dracula again!*'

Clark had a clean record, the paper reported, and was known not to touch alcohol. It was assumed that, for some reason he had climbed to the roof of the building, slipped and fallen.

Vaughan grimaced. This was not his idea of light reading before breakfast — and just why Ann thought they should investigate, he could not imagine.

He ordered breakfast for two and waited.

Ann Delmar arrived fifteen minutes later, looking as fresh as she always managed to look.

Vaughan growled: 'Some people don't seem to need sleep — and you can count me out of that group.'

She raised an eyebrow, and laughed.

'Why, Neil, I felt sure you were one of those athletic types who race around the block at the crack of dawn. You shouldn't disillusion a poor girl so!'

She had brought her own paper, a different one from Vaughan's and they compared the two stories. The few facts agreed, but each reporter had developed the horror aspect of it in his own way. Vaughan was fascinated and revolted.

'Well,' he began, 'what — '

But the arrival of breakfast postponed any discussion. Ann polished off bacon and eggs with an enthusiasm that made him wonder at her American nationality. The meal over, he sat back and regarded her quizzically.

'Now tell me why we should go to

Bankside,' he suggested.

'No reason,' she said. 'Just a hunch. We're looking for the solution to an impossible mystery. Giant bats are impossible. So my intuition tells me it's a lead to follow up.'

Vaughan crossed the room to the telephone and rang Scotland Yard. When he got through he asked for Superintendent Millet. There was a short pause, then —

'Hello, Neil. It's a long while since you bothered me — what is it this time? Nothing pleasant, I'll bet!'

'Can you give me any inside information on what happened at Bankside last night?'

The Superintendent sounded surprised.

'Don't tell me that M.I.5 are interested in giant bats!' A chuckle came from the receiver. 'You ought to know better than to place any credence in a newspaper story. What is this? A joke?'

'I'm serious,' Vaughan insisted. 'It may tie in with the case I'm working on.'

'Hold the line,' Millet said. 'I'll check with the officer in charge.'

Vaughan waited, turning to Ann.

'Bob Millet is an old friend of mine,' he explained, 'and it's useful having a personal contact at the Yard — saves a lot of time cutting through red tape.'

Millet came back.

'Sorry, Neil, I can't help you much. The facts are very few indeed and you've got them already from the papers. The general feeling here is that Clark met his death by accident.' A pause. 'Do you think it worth investigating?'

'I'd like to look at that empty building for myself. Can you arrange it?'

'Of course. I'll meet you there in twenty minutes. All right?'

'All right,' Vaughan said, and rang off. He looked at Ann. 'I hope this isn't going to be a wild-goose chase — Bob will never let me hear the end of it if we're wasting his time.'

They left the flat and Vaughan drove the Daimler through London's traffic. He crossed Southwark Bridge and swung right, moving parallel to the river. Ann pointed over a forest of masts to a majestic dome.

'That'll be St. Paul's, Neil?'

'That's right. Remind me to show you round sometime.'

He stopped the car as he saw Superintendent Millet standing by the curb, climbed out and shook hands with him.

'Bob, I want you to meet Ann Delmar, an American working with me.'

Millet smiled ruefully. He was between thirty and forty, clean-shaven with a fresh complexion and baby-blue eyes, and looked as unlike the conventional idea of a Scotland Yard man as it was possible to get.

'I'm in the wrong department, that's sure,' he grumbled. 'I never get anyone so glamorous working with me. It's a pleasure to meet you, Miss Delmar.'

They joined a police constable who was on duty at the entrance to the empty building, and went inside.

'I don't know what you expect to find,' Millet remarked casually, 'but whatever it is, I hope we can co-operate. I suppose you can't give me details of the job you're working on?'

Vaughan shook his head.

'Sorry, Bob. Not this time.'

The Superintendent grimaced.

'Not this time . . . not *any* time! You M.I5 people are as helpful as a blank wall.'

Vaughan stood looking about him. It had been a storeroom once, he assumed. There was a coating of dust on the floor and the walls were bare; high up, above the windows, rafters crossed from one side to the other.

'Something else turned up after you telephoned,' Millet said. 'The local station had to investigate this place — or rather, the man renting it — a few weeks back. It seems he took a lease on the building for twelve months and paid cash. The point is, he paid with stolen notes; stolen from a bank near here without leaving a trace! Mr. Smith — that's the name he gave — didn't leave a trace either. We still haven't located him.'

Vaughan and Ann exchanged glances, and she murmured:

'I think we're on to something.'

Vaughan studied the marks in the dust.

It was plain where Bill Clark and his dog had been; and he looked up to the high roof, speculating.

'If he fell, Bob . . . how the devil did he get up there in the first place?'

Millet sighed unhappily.

'I knew no good would come of this. Now I suppose the investigation will have to be re-opened. It's a good point, Neil. I can't see how he could have done it.'

Vaughan turned to the constable.

'I want to take a look up there,' he said. 'See if you can get a ladder from somewhere.'

The policeman went off and Vaughan nosed around.

'Clark came through from the warehouse yard. Why? What brought him here at all? You know, Bob, there are too many unexplained details to this set-up — I've a feeling you'll end up hunting a murderer.'

The constable came back, balancing a long ladder on his shoulder. Between them, they set it upright and Vaughan began to climb. Ann's words followed him upwards:

'What's that queer smell in here?'

He hadn't noticed it till then, but as he climbed, the smell became stronger — a peculiar, rancid odour. He reached the rafter against which the ladder was placed and peered about him. Dust and cobwebs, no sign of —

He stared at a section of the rafter a few feet away from him. Deep ridges had been gouged in it, as if by giant claws. There were more of them farther along. And on the next rafter.

Vaughan realized the marks were fresh and a cold chill swept through him. What had made those peculiar gouges in the woodwork? Bill Clark had talked of giant bats . . .

Abruptly, Vaughan didn't like the feeling of being up there, alone, amongst the rafters. He came down quicker than he had ascended.

'Well?' demanded Millet.

'There was some *thing* up there,' Vaughan said grimly. 'And recently. You'll want experts for this one, Bob. And I don't think you're going to like what you find!'

* * *

Irwin was wearing a track in his office carpet when Vaughan and Ann arrived, in answer to an urgent summons, and the movement of his small feet had lost its dancing quality. He moved more like a caged tiger and his face showed worry.

Vaughan said: 'More uranium missing?'

'Not uranium.' Irwin sat down abruptly, tired, his age showing. 'Silver.' He held up one hand and marked off the items on his fingers. 'Tin.' A long sigh. 'Copper.'

Vaughan dropped into a seat; he felt bewildered. Irwin glanced at a paper on his desk and spoke.

'I've only just heard about this new development. A transport plane was flying a load of silver bullion from the refinery, in British Columbia, to Ottawa. It was a non-stop flight. The metal was checked aboard. There was a crew of three and two guards. On arrival at Ottawa, it was found that the silver had gone. Somehow, it disappeared in *mid-flight*!'

Ann suggested: 'It could have been

dropped overboard.'

Irwin shook his head.

'All the men involved are above suspicion. Besides, there are other disappearances. A valuable shipment of pure tin, locked in a strongroom, under guard. When it was wanted, it just wasn't there. That happened in Malaysia.'

Vaughan and Ann exchanged glances. The description of something that might have been a 'flying saucer' had come from Malaysia.

'And in Zimbabwe,' Irwin went on. 'It is copper. A very large quantity, so I understand — of refined ore. It was stored in a warehouse and vanished one night.'

Vaughan felt cautiously around the idea.

'You think there's a connection?'

'If there isn't, coincidence is stretching a very long arm indeed!'

No one spoke for some minutes. A clock ticked loudly into the silence.

Irwin cleared his throat.

'What it amounts to is this. Throughout the world important raw materials are disappearing in fantastic circumstances. Uranium, silver, tin, copper — all basic requirements to civilized society as we know it. Suppose the losses continue . . . what is going to happen?'

Vaughan shifted uneasily.

'I suppose we'll get to the bottom of it before things go too far.'

Irwin looked at him, and his voice dropped to a whisper.

'And if we don't . . . '

Vaughan's imagination started playing tricks. A world without atomic power — and the reserves of coal and oil being rapidly used up. Electrical industry breaking down for lack of copper and silver. Food shortages in over-populated cities caused by lack of tinplate for canning the seasonal gluts. Take away a few essential raw materials and there was no telling what would be the result.

He put a brake on his runaway thoughts.

'We're letting the problem get out of proportion,' he said. 'All right, the position is serious — but it's not the end of the world. The thing that has us baffled is the apparent impossibility of the circumstances in which the materials have vanished. We'll solve that before long . . . then it will be an easy step to find a defence against further losses.'

Irwin said: 'I suppose you're right,' and picked up another sheet of paper. 'Something for you, Miss Delmar. I asked the Astronomer Royal to keep a watch on the night skies — and he turned up with this. An elliptical black shadow that crossed the moon and changed direction half-way across!'

Vaughan was slower than the girl in spotting the implication of the statement.

She burst out: 'No natural body could do that!'

'Exactly. No *natural* body . . . '

Vaughan remembered the file of newspaper cuttings that Rubenstein had collected — more than a hundred of them, relating to strange objects seen in the sky — and a nervous thrill shot through him. It began to seem increasingly unlikely that foreign governments were involved in this business.

'Message for Miss Delmar,' said young Rubenstein, putting his head round the door. 'From Washington.'

Ann took the document and examined it.

'Coded,' she said briefly. 'Excuse me, Neil — this may be important.'

They were once more at the headquarters of M.I.5. Vaughan nodded, going through a fresh batch of cuttings. The buzzer of the inter-office communication system sounded and he answered it.

'Yes . . . right . . . I'll come along now.' He switched off. 'Irwin wants us again, Ann — follow on when you're through.'

She nodded abstractedly as she worked at decoding the message.

Vaughan walked along the passage under the light of fluorescent tubes, the purring of ventilation motors in the background. This building reminded him in some ways — the bare white walls, the dustless corners — of a hospital. But a hospital would have windows on to the outside world; here, there was a feeling of tension, of being cut off, something apart from the bustling traffic a couple of hundred yards away. In the centre of London, he might have been on another planet.

He knocked on the door of Irwin's office and walked in.

'Sit down, Neil,' Irwin said. 'I have three more items for you. First, a bar of silver has been found and identified as coming from the bullion stolen in mid-air over Canada. Listen to this eyewitness account:

'I, Joseph Henry Smith, was fishing from the southern bank of Cree Lake, Saskatchewan, early on Friday morning. It was perfectly quiet and there was no one about. The sky was absolutely clear and I did not hear any sounds of aircraft. I could not say what caused me to look up, but I did, and saw something falling towards me. It glittered in the sunlight. When the object hit the ground, some yards from me, I saw that it was a bar of silver. I studied the sky carefully, but saw no aircraft from which it could have fallen. I took the bar of silver to the police depot at Prince Albert, and registered my find.'

'Cree Lake,' Irwin added, 'is roughly one hundred miles north of the route which the plane took from the refinery to Ottawa. How do you explain that?'

Vaughan couldn't explain it.

'How many bars of silver was the plane carrying?' he asked.

'Twenty-five.'

And one had fallen from an empty sky, a hundred miles away. It smacked of black magic.

'Second item.' Irwin handed him a sheet of notepaper headed: *Unusual Bat Behaviour*. The byline was that of Clifford Nash, a well-known naturalist. Nash had written: 'Last night I was in a wood to the south of Dunstead village, with the object of studying bat behaviour. Up until one-thirty a.m., I saw nothing of note. Then, quite suddenly, the wood became alive with bats in the most extraordinary way. They came past me in a swarm, flying fast and erratically, and emitting high-pitched squeaks of alarm. Something had certainly scared them to alight, but though I searched the wood thoroughly, I could not discover what had driven them to this state of panic. I kept watch until dawn, but the bats did not return. The only other thing I noted was a peculiar rancid odour, reminiscent of the bats themselves, but much stronger. I have never known bats to behave in such a manner before.'

Vaughan noted the location; Dunstead — and thought Nash had been lucky not to encounter the reason for the bats' flight.

Irwin waited for him to finish reading before he continued:

'The third item is this: Russia has just resigned from the United Nations. In a short and un-illuminating speech, the Soviet delegate accused the western powers of sabotaging his country's resources. He did not give any specific instances of this alleged sabotage, and withdrew from the chamber immediately.'

Vaughan whistled softly.

'Then Russia, too, may be suffering the same sort of losses as we are — '

'Or pulling a bluff,' Irwin cut in, 'to hide their own activities.'

'I wonder . . . '

The door opened and Ann entered the room. She had a sheet of paper in her hand, on which she had written the decoded message.

'I'm leaving for home immediately,' she said, handing over the paper. 'You might as well read the latest development.'

Irwin took the message and read it, passing it to Vaughan.

DELMAR: REPORT TO WASHINGTON. GOLD BULLION MISSING FROM FORT KNOX. CIRCUMSTANCES SIMILAR TO URANIUM THEFTS. SUSPECT SAME AGENCY. STOKES.

Vaughan said: 'Uranium — silver — tin — copper. And now gold! What the devil is going on?'

Even Irwin was shaken by the news. He ran one hand through his graying hair in a gesture of helplessness.

'This is the most impossible of all . . . to take gold from the American reserve! The most impregnable treasure vault ever constructed — it defies the imagination.'

Ann had already collected her papers and briefcase and was ready to leave.

'Will you run me to London airport, Neil? And Mr. Irwin, will you phone through to hold me a seat on the first plane leaving for the States?'

Irwin nodded, reaching for an outside telephone as Vaughan escorted her to the door. He called after them:

'Good luck, Miss Delmar — and good hunting!'

Vaughan drove Ann to the *Royal*, where it took her only a few minutes to pack her suitcase, then on to London airport. The big Daimler ate up the miles. Vaughan felt unhappy; though he had not known Ann Delmar very long, the thought of losing her so soon depressed him.

He said, without taking his eyes off the road ahead: 'We've got to meet again, Ann. Keep in touch, and I'll join you as soon as this business is over.'

She smiled, nestling close to him.

'I feel the same way, Neil. We mustn't

lose touch. Anyway, I have a hunch we'll be running across each other before we solve this problem. All leads must converge on one point — somewhere.'

The rest of the journey was made in silence. Vaughan had a lot of things he wanted to say to her, but the words would not come. Already, he was beginning to feel an insignificant cog in the events sweeping across the world. His personal problem was lost in the greater one.

He turned off the Bath Road as the airfield came into view. He drove to the terminal; in the distance, broad concrete runways stretched to the horizon. The noise of aircraft engines filled the air.

In the reception hall, a clerk waited with tickets.

'Miss Delmar?' Ann showed her documentation. The clerk nodded. 'A plane is waiting for you. On instructions from London, we have held up the takeoff a few minutes. Will you please go aboard at once?' She pushed the tickets into her pocket.

'Au revoir, Neil . . . '

He realized she was waiting for

something — and took her in his arms as if that were the most natural thing in the world. His lips pressed against hers in a long kiss. When she broke away, she was smiling in a satisfied way.

'Thank you, Neil.'

Then she was walking to the van waiting to take her to the plane. The sunlight glinted on her blonde head as she waved back. The van moved off passing quickly from sight.

Minutes later, he heard the note of aircraft engines change. A four-jet transport glided along the runway and climbed into the air. It grew rapidly smaller, became a dot in the bright blue of the sky, and finally vanished completely.

Neil Vaughan turned back to his car, disturbingly conscious of the lingering perfume that still clung to his jacket.

5

Fort Knox

It was late when Vaughan headed back for London. After seeing Ann off at the airport, he drove aimlessly in a wide circle; he had many things on his mind and had long since discovered that he thought best while driving. So he avoided main roads and kept his speed down to thirty as he threaded a way through sprawling suburbs.

It began to rain. He switched on the windscreen wipers and dropped speed. The Daimler's headlights cut a bright channel through the darkness and rain, while the wipers lulled him with their monotonous rhythm.

He wondered what really had happened at Dunstead — it seemed impossible that uranium 235 could have been taken out of the plant by any human agency, yet his scientific training rebelled against a supernatural explanation. And it wasn't only uranium; silver, tin, and copper were missing. Gold too. Thinking about Fort Knox brought Ann Delmar back to mind . . . when would he see her again?

He checked his thoughts. He must keep his mind on the job. What connection was there between Bill Clark's mysterious death and Rubenstein's list of 'flying saucer' stories? Or between those ridges deeply gouged in the rafters of a deserted building and the odd behaviour of bats noted by Clifford Nash?

Vaughan sighed heavily. The whole thing was 'nuts'.

Ahead, the shining black surface of the road fell away in a gentle slope. He had the vague idea that he was somewhere near Ealing, driving downhill between ranks of tall, closely-planted trees, their foliage blocking out all light except that given by his headlamps.

Then, abruptly, through the blurring rain and the arcing wipers, he saw the figure of a man directly in front of him. Vaughan stamped on the footbrake and swung the wheel in a desperate attempt to miss the lonely pedestrian.

The car skidded sideways on the wet surface and Vaughan released the brake to regain control. The engine roared. Trees and road and pedestrian whirled crazily . . . he swung the wheel again but the Daimler's tyres were spinning uselessly. He was going to crash.

The trunk of a tree loomed up . . . Vaughan made himself relax — and looked quickly for the man in the road. Had he hit him? A tall figure stood to one side.

Seeing it, shock stabbed Vaughan with almost physical impact. What he saw was no man . . .

He had a glimpse of immense wings spreading out, a lifting body. Then the thing flapped off into the night.

The next moment the car rammed a massive tree trunk . . .

★ ★ ★

When Ann Delmar landed at New York there was a plane waiting to take her direct to Washington. She had expected that, but all the same, she would have enjoyed spending an hour or two with her parents at their Long Island home. Working for the American Intelligence it was often several months before she saw them.

The plane flew southwest, over Trenton and the Delaware River, with Philadelphia sprawling out below. Chesapeake Bay came into view, sparkling blue water dotted with triangular white sails. Baltimore was away to her right just visible as a dark blur through the clouds.

Ann sat with her briefcase on her lap, but her mind was not on its contents. She was remembering Neil Vaughan, and the way she had wanted to kiss him. And, partly for that reason, she was not looking forward to the interview at Washington.

The plane began to descend. From the window, Ann saw a grass field cut crisscross with concrete runways and the rows of sheds round the perimeter. Gentle as a bird, the plane glided in to land, touched down, and taxied up to the disembarkation point.

A fast car was waiting. Ann settled back in her seat as the car travelled through wide avenues lined with trees; she saw the domed Capitol in the distance and crossed the Potomac. And she wondered what Stokes would say when she told him about Neil Vaughan.

Fifteen minutes later, she arrived at Intelligence Headquarters, showed her identification and passed inside. Stokes, head of the department for which Ann worked, was in his office — a tall, distinguished man of forty, dressed in a dark pin-stripe suit.

He stepped forward to greet her, smiling and holding out his hand; his manner was warmer than that of an executive greeting a department worker. His face lit up with pleasure at the sight of her.

'Hello, Ann, it's nice to see you again. You can't imagine how dull this office has been since you left.'

'Hello, Richard.' She avoided his eyes, dropping the briefcase on the table and opening it. She handed him a sheaf of papers. 'My report. I'm afraid you won't find much of use.'

He turned the pages quickly, scanning the summary notes she had appended. Then he locked the report in his desk.

'I'll go through it later,' he said. 'We're flying out to Fort Knox. My men have been over the place without turning up anything. I put off my own visit till you got back — I thought you might have discovered something to give us a lead.'

'Was much taken?' Ann asked.

Stokes frowned.

'Gold bullion worth billions of dollars. The President is badly worried — nothing like this has happened before.'

He looked at her sharply.

'Are you ready to travel?'

She nodded.

He picked up a phone, gave orders to someone unseen, then took her arm. Outside a car waited.

'The airport,' Stokes told the driver, and settled back. 'What sort of trip did you have?'

'All right.' She didn't feel like talking. There was something she had to say, but she wanted to be alone with him.

The pilot took off, heading west over Virginia. And Ann found herself alone with Stokes in a soundproof cabin.

Abruptly, she spoke, her eyes averted from him.

'Richard, before I left, you asked me to marry you. I said I wasn't sure how I felt. I am now . . . I can't marry you.'

He stared at her, hard lines tightening the corners of his mouth. He fumbled for words.

'Something happened? Over there?'

'Yes. I met someone. Richard — please try to understand, it's something I can't help. I don't mean to hurt you . . . '

Charleston was below them, a dot on the landscape.

Stokes lit a cigarette and expelled the smoke from his lungs in a slow, deliberate stream.

'I guess there's nothing I can say, except that I hope he makes you happy, Ann.'

'Thank you. It would be best if I were transferred to another department.'

He shook his head.

'Sorry, Ann, but I need you on this job.

There isn't anyone who can take over at short notice — and this is important. Perhaps the most important thing we've ever had to tackle.'

'Very well,' she said.

Silence fell between them. The Kentucky landscape moved panoramically beneath the plane. Ann gazed out of the window, feeling miserable because she'd had to hurt a man she both liked and respected. Stokes crushed out his cigarette and sighed heavily. They were two people who had to start their lives all over again, on a different footing.

She was glad when Fort Knox came into view. It gave her something else to think about. The job came first, and personal feelings could be suppressed.

The plane angled down, aiming for an airfield alongside the army reservation. Fort Knox was a square building with a gun turret at each corner; light glinted on the barrels of the guns as they moved to cover the approach of the plane. Armed soldiers patrolled the electrified fence surrounding the fort. And, Ann knew, there were hidden other more sophisticated electronic defences.

Below ground, in deep vaults, was the United States gold reserve — billions of dollars in bullion. Ann was remembering the words of an official report she had once read: 'Fort Knox is bombproof and burglarproof.' Or so it had seemed . . .

The plane landed. An army captain with an escort of ten men marched up. He inspected their passes and took them through the steel gates into the fortress. There were soldiers everywhere; in the passages, at the locked doors between each section, at the lift shafts dropping down to the vaults.

The Commandant had a row of medals across his chest, a walrus moustache and eyes that seemed to bore through anyone he looked at.

'Wondered when you would show up, Stokes,' he said, 'though I don't know what you can do. There's nothing to suggest how the gold might have been removed . . . if I didn't find it hard not to believe my own eyes, I'd say it was impossible. But the stuff's gone — one vault cleaned right out.'

Stokes answered: 'I'd have been here before, only I was waiting for Miss Delmar.' The Commandant nodded curtly at Ann. 'She has been working on a similar case, without learning much, I'm afraid. This is a very serious affair. There has been more than one — ah — disappearance of this kind.'

'This one is serious enough for me,' the Commandant said sourly, 'I suppose you want to go below?'

Stokes nodded, a little stiffly. The Commandant had a poor opinion of the Secret Service.

They dropped into the bowels of the earth in a lift-cage. At the bottom, concrete tunnels branched out to the various vaults; each was constructed of torch-proof steel, locked and barred and guarded by soldiers. The tunnels were isolated from each other by more steel doors. Set in the ceiling of the tunnels, lenses and grilles hinted at closed-circuit television and narcotic gas outlets.

At each checkpoint, Ann and Stokes — the Commandant too — had to show special passes. Photoelectric eyes watched their progress. Hidden cameras recorded their every step. Ann thought: this is fantastic — no one could break in here, never mind take gold out!

They reached the door of the vault that had been robbed. Soldiers opened the massive steel door and they passed inside. The door closed again.

Two of Stokes' men sat staring gloomily at nothing, their expressions revealing how little they had learnt. They made their report on how much was missing and in what form, the precautions that had been in existence at the time, and the steps that had been taken to discover how the gold had vanished.

'I suppose,' the Commandant said tersely, 'you are trying to prove that my men are involved in this theft?'

Both agents denied this strenuously, and one turned to Stokes.

'Suppose that we assume the guards are involved.' He consulted a list of names. 'Twenty-seven men would be concerned, between here and the outside wall. Considering that the men are changed round on their shifts, no two working together at any set time, the planning of a robbery would be sheer fantasy, apart from the fact that such a quantity of bullion would be seen, anyway.'

Ann inspected the vault. The heavy steel walls, floor and roof were untouched. Anyone who had entered must have done so by the door . . . and that was clearly impossible. She was reminded of an empty store shed at Dunstead.

'There's nothing for us here,' Stokes said. 'Let's get back to the surface.'

The Commandant was almost laughing.

'It's your worry now, Stokes,' he said. 'My responsibility ends when the gold leaves here — and that seems to have happened. I wish you the best of luck!'

Stokes checked the outside wall and covered the ground surrounding the fort. He learnt precisely nothing. At night searchlights played on the electric fence; no one could have got through without sounding an alarm. He sighed.

'This is a real headache, Ann . . . we're

up against something superhuman!'

Ann hardly heard him. She was looking at the sky and wondering what had been up there when the gold disappeared from Fort Knox. And she wondered if they would ever learn the truth about these fantastic disappearances.

6

The Photograph

Neil Vaughan woke up in bed with his head pounding like a trip-hammer and no memory of what had happened. It was some minutes before his eyes focused properly and his brain stopped its mad whirl. Then he saw the plain cream walls, the table by his side with its array of bottles and ointments, and smelled the particular smell that a hospital exudes.

He began to remember; the drive through London; the man that was not a man; the crash. He wondered how much time had passed and whether Irwin knew he was here. He sat up, intending to get out of bed, but sudden pain shot through his head and he fell back again.

He tried more cautiously a second time, sitting up, and looking about him. His clothes had been taken away. There was a mirror on the bedside table and he

83

picked it up and looked at his reflection. The top of his head was swathed in bandages and strips of plaster covered his cheeks.

He was in a small private ward and there was a bell-push in the wall at his back. He leant across and pressed it. A nurse came in, found him half-out of bed and promptly pushed him back again.

'You can't get up yet,' she said. 'The doctor will be in to see you presently — till then you must rest.'

'Does anyone know I'm here?' Vaughan asked.

'A Mr. Rubenstein called. He said he would be back later.'

The nurse left him. Vaughan thought: someone at the hospital had gone through his pockets, found his identification and got in touch with Irwin.

Time passed. Vaughan began to feel hungry — also impatient to be on his feet again.

Rubenstein came in.

'Hello, Mr. Vaughan,' the younger man said. 'I'm sorry to see you like this. Mr. Irwin said you're not to worry; he can look after things till you're well again.'

'You tell him I'll be out of here as soon as I get these wrappings off and my hands on my clothes! Any news?'

Rubenstein sat on the chair at Vaughan's bed.

'Mr. Irwin said I was to tell you that he'd gone down to Dunstead, and would call here on the way back. And I've some newspapers for you to read.'

He brought a bundle of dailies from his briefcase and spread them on the bed. The headlines hit Vaughan.

SOVIET WAR THREAT
RUSSIA ACCUSES WESTERN
POWERS OF SABOTAGE

Why has Russia left the United Nations? Are the powers behind the iron curtain preparing for a third world war, as some authorities seem to think? The United States is reported to be calling up more men for the armed forces . . .

Vaughan read quickly through the newspaper stories. Nothing new had occurred; the journalists were playing up

Russia's withdrawal from the United Nations in a big way, making a mountain out of a molehill. Perhaps they were right — Vaughan didn't feel sure. Suppose the Russians, too, were losing uranium and other metals? What then?

'Anything I can get you?' Rubenstein asked.

'Apart from getting me out of here — no.'

Rubenstein took his departure, and a few minutes later the doctor arrived. He was a young man with a long jaw and slender hands, and he smiled at Vaughan.

'How are you feeling now?'

Vaughan said: 'Hungry.'

The doctor began unfastening the bandages about his head, talking all the while.

'I understand there's some pressure being exerted to have you released from here. That's as may be; my job is to make you fit again, and I can't do that if you're running around loose.'

He removed the last bandage, peered into Vaughan's face and gently pressed his skull with his fingers.

'Hurt?'

Vaughan set his teeth. 'No.'

'H'm.' The doctor felt carefully round his head. 'You had a lucky escape. There's nothing broken. Some skin gone, and a nasty cut, but it'll heal well enough. It would be best if you stayed here two or three days.'

Vaughan said: 'That's out of the question.'

'You were delirious when they brought you in,' the doctor remarked casually. 'Rambling away about a man who turned into a giant bat and flew off. Remember anything about it?'

'I don't remember.'

'Well, you can have a meal now. And the nurse will give you something to make you sleep. By then your headache will have gone.'

A nurse brought him food on a tray. Vaughan ate hungrily; finished up with a glass of water and two sleeping tablets, and sank into slumber.

He woke up feeling better. He could sit up without getting any sharp pain in his head. The mirror showed that he still had a bandage round his forehead and a strip of adhesive plaster down one cheek.

The door opened and a nurse announced:

'A visitor for you, Mr. Vaughan.'

It was a worried-looking Irwin who came into the room.

'Hello, Neil. Feeling better?'

'Better than I look! What's happened while I've been out of things?'

'Plenty.' Irwin sat down, heavily, with the air of a man who feels his responsibility. 'There was a call for you from Dunstead. Unfortunately, there was some delay before the department found out you were in hospital and the message was passed to me.' He took a deep breath. 'I got there too late to do anything.'

Vaughan tensed.

'They had prepared another batch of 235, and stored it, under guard. Professor Stanley remained *inside* the shed — with a camera. When I got there, the uranium — and Stanley — had disappeared!'

'No one saw anything?' Vaughan asked.

Irwin sighed.

'No. The storeroom was surrounded

and closely watched Stanley went in, and didn't come out — he just vanished, along with the uranium.'

'And the camera?'

Vaughan was excited. It was obvious that Stanley had waited hoping to get pictures of whatever happened at the moment of disappearance. Had he succeeded? What had the scientist seen?

'The camera was found on the floor, slightly damaged — as if Stanley dropped it hurriedly. Perhaps he had a severe shock.' Irwin paused. 'Perhaps we will never learn what happened. It was an ordinary box camera holding a roll-film — and one frame had been exposed. I had it developed on the spot . . . and that is the craziest part of all!'

He opened his wallet and handed Vaughan a print.

'What do you make of this?'

Vaughan looked at the photograph. The background showed one wall, and part of a steel rack loaded with aluminium canisters. *The uranium had still been in the store when Stanley clicked the shutter.* But it was the animal in the foreground that held his attention.

It was a bat, with wings unfolding, facing the camera. The eyes were small, the ears short, the body covered with fur. But it was the size of the thing that got under Vaughan's skin — he made an effort to judge the scale remembering the height of the bench in the Dunstead storeroom and reckoned it to be around seven feet tall.

He stared, fascinated.

Irwin said. 'It gets you, doesn't it? I've looked at that picture until I think I'm going out of my mind. It doesn't make sense, however I look at it. Johns thinks the picture is a fake, a red herring to throw us off the scent. He believes Stanley is responsible for taking the uranium.'

'And how does he explain the disappearing act?' Vaughan asked.

Irwin shrugged. 'He doesn't explain it.'

Vaughan picked up the photograph and studied it again.

'I haven't told you yet how I came to crash into a tree,' he said grimly. 'I saw this thing — or one of them. It looked to me just like a man standing in the road then . . . it *changed*. This picture is no fake, I can swear to that.'

His thoughts turned to Professor Stanley. Where was the scientist now?

Irwin grunted. 'I don't like this at all. What sort of hellish business are we getting into?'

Vaughan swung his legs out of bed and stood upright. He walked about the room. He felt all right, a little dizzy perhaps, but he wasn't going to collapse.

'Hunt up my clothes,' he said. 'I'm going to pay a visit to Regent's Park. Perhaps someone at the zoo can throw a little light on this . . . this damned bat!'

Minutes later, dressed, Vaughan walked out of the hospital, despite protests from the sister-in-charge. Irwin returned to his office, to see if any new developments had occurred, while Vaughan took a taxi to Regent's Park.

He made his way through the zoological gardens, to the superintendent's office. He showed his identification and requested that the subject of his visit remain confidential; then he produced the photograph that Irwin had brought from Dunstead.

'Can you identify this creature for me? Or tell me anything about it at all?'

The superintendent studied the picture. He was a portly man with a bulbous nose and shaggy eyebrows. He grunted a couple of times, took a magnifying glass from his desk drawer and continued to stare solemnly at the photograph, turning it first one way, then another.

'A remarkable creature,' he said finally. 'Do you have the — er — original, Mr. Vaughan? No? Well perhaps you can tell me where the picture was taken — In this country? H'm . . . '

'Is it a bat?' Vaughan asked abruptly.

The superintendent hesitated.

'It *looks* like a bat,' he replied cautiously. 'Do you object if one of my assistants sees this?'

Vaughan didn't object. He badly needed information.

The superintendent picked up the house telephone. 'Switchboard? Please find Mr. Parkins for me, and ask him to report to my office immediately.'

He replaced the phone, stood looking into space, then turned to Vaughan.

'Parkins is keeper of the small mammal house,' he explained, 'and bats belong to that family. I doubt if there is a better authority on bats, in this country than Parkins.'

They waited in silence, Vaughan restless, the superintendent absorbed in his study of the animal that appeared to be a giant bat. Then he looked up.

'I am not a very good host, Mr. Vaughan. Will you take a glass of sherry? And please sit down.'

Vaughan tried the sherry and found it surprisingly good.

Parkins arrived, thin and uniformed, looking rather like one of the small mammals he maintained, and smelling of them. He, too, studied the photograph. Vaughan sipped his sherry and waited for the experts to speak.

Parkins wanted to know where the animal was, and if Vaughan had it in his possession.

'I wish I had! Gentlemen, I can tell you

nothing. I want your opinion on this photograph.'

Parkins cleared his throat.

'It looks, superficially, like *Nyctalus leisleri* — but there are differences . . . '

'Ah!' said the superintendent, nodding. 'You see the same thing. A new species, would you say?'

'Undoubtedly. Notice it stands? I know of no species which can stand.'

'And the size of it!'

'The expression of the face is unusually intelligent.'

'The feet — '

'Yes! Almost hands . . . with a thumb-like grip. Quite remarkable.'

Vaughan interrupted: 'Am I to understand that this bat is something new? Like no other animal — ' and he emphasized the last phrase — '*on this Earth?*'

The superintendent and Parkins agreed.

'That is our considered opinion, Mr. Vaughan.'

There was a long silence. Vaughan finished his sherry, collected the photograph and prepared to leave.

'Naturally, we should like to know more,' the superintendent said. 'If you need help in capturing the creature, I hope you will come to us. We should be most happy to receive a specimen for the zoo.'

'There's nothing I'd like better! I only hope it will be possible . . . '

Vaughan left the superintendent's office and walked about the gardens. He walked aimlessly, thinking. What had he discovered? Missing metal. Lights in the sky. A giant bat. The pieces of the jigsaw would not fit, no matter how he shuffled them. And there was Stanley. The professor was the one man who really knew what had happened in the uranium store at Dunstead.

It became suddenly imperative that Stanley be found. They must throw secrecy out of the window now; a nation-wide hunt should be started at once. The police would have to be informed, ports and airfields watched. Stanley *must* be found!

Vaughan quickened his step. He would see Irwin immediately and get the search organized. He looked about him for an exit from the zoo — and saw a signpost, inscribed:

To the Small Mammal House.

Vaughan realized that he had never seen a bat close to, and had a sudden urge to do so. He followed the direction of the signpost.

The bats had a large cage to themselves. There were a dozen of them, hanging upside down from the wire-mesh roof; one spread its wings and glided diagonally across the cage. Ugly brutes, Vaughan thought — and tried to imagine one standing seven feet high. He shuddered.

He smelled the rancid odour he had noticed in the empty building where Bill Clark had died, and studied them more closely. The fur had a silky texture and the wings spread between elongated forefingers and joined to the ankles and tail. The toes were clawed.

The bats regarded him with bright, beady eyes, sometimes gliding across the cage, sometimes attending to their toilet — they were scrupulous in the attention to their fur. Vaughan racked his brain for such information as he had about bats, and found it surprisingly little. They hunted at night and possessed the miraculous gift of echo-location; by emitting bursts of supersonic vibration, they could fly in the dark without hitting obstacles. It was a kind of natural radar.

He took out the photograph again, comparing the creature in the picture with the bats in the cage. Yes, there *were* differences . . .

He turned away, left Regent's Park, and hired a taxi to drive him to the block of offices that acted as a cover for Military Intelligence. He paid off the cab and went directly to Irwin's office.

Briefly, he reported the superintendent's views on the giant bat and suggested a hunt for Stanley.

Irwin sighed, picking up a message-form from the table and crumpling it between his hands.

'Stanley's been found — dead! So he can tell us nothing. He was still wearing the white uniform he would have put on to visit the uranium store. His body was found on the Sussex Downs, some miles away, and looked as if it had fallen from a great height — mangled almost beyond recognition.'

Vaughan thought of a bar of silver that had fallen from an empty sky.

'There is no doubt it was the professor?' he asked.

'None.'

Vaughan paced the room, hands thrust deep in his pockets.

'It tells us one thing — whoever is behind the uranium thefts is not going to stop at murder. Stanley found out something — so he had to die.'

'Here's something else.' Irwin handed him a duplicated bulletin that had been sent in from a news agency. 'If this report is correct, well, I don't know what to think.'

The item was headed: *Brodsk, Tuesday*. 'The mysterious disappearance of a large amount of copper from a factory on the outskirts of the town is being investigated by police.

'About one hundred employees have been stood off by the management as no work is available for them until fresh stocks are obtained. The factory produces electrical equipment.'

Irwin waited until he had finished reading, then said:

'Brodsk is behind the what we used to call the Iron Curtain — which the Russians might now be re-introducing.'

Vaughan didn't like it. Right up to that moment, he had fought his growing suspicion that some non-human agency was at work. But Brodsk was in a satellite state of Russia — and the Russians would hardly rob their own stocks.

He stood quite still, looking at Irwin.

'If only we knew for certain,' he growled. 'We've got to be sure — and there's only one way to find out. I'm going to Moscow to investigate!'

7

Moscow

It was not quite as easy as that. Irwin didn't like the idea, and said so.

'Suppose the Russians are responsible, and planning war against the west . . . then you'll walk straight into a trap and spend the rest of your life in a Siberian mine.'

Vaughan talked him into putting it before the Prime Minister; the interview was short — and Vaughan got his way.

Again there was delay. Time was important. So a R.A.F. jet-plane was commandeered, with two pilots to exchange duties and Vaughan the only passenger.

They took off at sunset, flying due east across the channel and Holland. As dawn approached, the plane nosed down through the clouds, passing over miles of open farmland to the capital city of the

Soviet Republic. At the airport officials were waiting for him. His credentials were examined, then he was driven into the city in a big black saloon. As they crossed the Moskva river his interpreter — a blonde-haired, buxom woman — said:

'You are being taken to the Kremlin where an interview will be granted.'

Her name, Vaughan learnt, was Fedora. She was an unsmiling, uncommunicative woman who kept her translations brief and ventured no comment of her own.

Vaughan watched everything from the car window, interested, for this was his first visit. To him, Moscow appeared primarily a city of contrasts; a mixture of ancient and modern, the beautiful and the ugly. The river was spanned by noble bridges, blocks of flats were concrete and glass, an entrance to the Underground railway black and pink and pearly-grey marble — while shabby, narrow alleys led to dark and dingy dwelling houses waiting to be torn down and rebuilt.

The towers of the Kremlin, rising like stern watchdogs, conflicted with the

101

oriental splendour of a cathedral's cupolas. He saw an officer of the Red Army, resplendent in a spotless uniform; and workmen dressed in cheap, shoddy clothes.

The car moved across the Red Square, to the Kremlin itself. Vaughan began to wonder what his reception would be. Friendly . . . or suspicious?

He was escorted to a room and asked, politely, to wait. He sat down with Fedora. He asked her questions to which he got monosyllabic answers. She seemed a woman of little conversation and even less curiosity.

Vaughan waited a long time. Perhaps the officials in the Kremlin were unsure how to handle him; or were making arrangements for his eventual disappearance; perhaps they were simply embarrassed by a visit from a member of British Intelligence.

He wandered across to a window and stared out over the Red Square. The sun was rising over distant minarets and smoke drifted in grey plumes from factory chimneys. Buses and other vehicles were carrying people to work. A mass of flowers added a note of colour to a park set between the terminus of the Trans-Siberian railway and an old, grim-walled palace.

Vaughan turned from the window. Fedora watched him closely; and behind her, a huge mirror set in a gilded frame showed Vaughan as he must appear to these people — tall and rugged, his thick black beard jutting forward and a bandage about his head.

He said, loudly: 'I'd like some food,' and wondered if he would be allowed to leave.

Fedora passed on his request, and, some little while later, a tray was brought in; soup, with veal rissoles and cauliflower, ice cream and coffee. Vaughan ate, and relaxed.

The double-doors opened and two men entered; the first said something in Russian, looking at Vaughan, a fixed smile on his face. Fedora translated:

'You will come with us.'

They went down a tiled passage, dark, the only light coming from narrow windows set high in the walls. The room at the end was brilliantly lit and steaming with heat. Six men sat round a circular table with papers in front of them. Conversation stopped as Vaughan entered, and they all stared at him.

Vaughan sat down at the table, in a chair indicated to him. Fedora stayed; his escort left, closing the door.

'You are before members of the government and representatives of the Intelligence service,' Fedora explained briefly.

Vaughan's eyes were drawn to one man in particular; he was huge, wrapped in a thick fur coat, and had the appearance of a great, shaggy bear. His gaze settled on Vaughan's face and never left it during the interview that followed; he was the only one who did not speak.

'You are Neil Vaughan, of the British Intelligence service?'

'Yes.'

Vaughan began to realize how long-drawn out this was going to be, with every question and answer translated through Fedora.

'Why have you come?'

'I am investigating the loss of certain valuable metals. I understand that you may have suffered similar losses. Is that true?'

He did not get an answer immediately. The Russians talked volubly amongst themselves but Fedora did not translate. A question was shot at him:

'These losses — what are they? And where?'

Vaughan replied, through Fedora: 'Uranium 235. Tin. Silver. Copper. The losses occurred in Britain, Malaya, Canada and Rhodesia. Uranium and gold are missing from the United States.'

More animated talk that Vaughan could not follow. The Russians seemed excited, arguing with each other. The man in the fur coat remained aloof, watching Vaughan intently.

He was challenged: 'How do we know you speak the truth?'

Vaughan pulled a sheaf of papers from his pocket and spread them on the table before him. The top sheet was a letter signed by the Prime Minister, stating that

Neil Vaughan, Special Agent, was acting with full authority of the British Government. The other papers summarized the incidents at Dunstead and elsewhere.

Even though Fedora spoke rapidly, it took her some minutes to get over the basic material to her countrymen. When she finished, there was a long silence.

Vaughan waited anxiously. He couldn't force the Russians to co-operate. He could only hope . . .

'Why have you come to us? Suppose that we admit to losing some of our stocks, what then?'

Vaughan leaned forward, talking at the man in the fur coat.

'Some people in the west blame you. And I don't doubt that you suspect Britain and America if you have lost important stocks of raw material — but I can assure you that we are not responsible. On the contrary, the British and American governments are worried by their own losses. The point is, if — as I suspect — you are investigating a series of mysterious disappearances in your own country, well . . .'

His voice tailed off. Fedora prompted: 'If we are — what then?'

Vaughan could no longer evade the answer that had been slowly building up at the back of his mind. He had to face it.

'Then the whole world is threatened by beings from another planet!'

He sat back, suddenly released from tension. He felt better now that he'd said it. After a moment's silence the Russians began to talk animatedly. A sharp-featured man was gesticulating, stabbing his forefinger at Vaughan and spitting words. Fedora did not bother to interpret.

Eventually, they all looked to the man in the fur coat for guidance. He did not speak, merely nodded.

Fedora said: 'It is true, we have lost stocks of uranium 235, and copper and tin. Our investigations have led nowhere; we do not understand how the metals have vanished.'

Vaughan felt cold, his body tense. It was true, then . . . there could be no other explanation. Beings from another world were plundering the resources of Earth!

Fedora began to translate papers that

were handed to her, and Vaughan learnt the extent of the Soviet losses. Uranium 235 headed the list; already they had been forced to shut down two atomic piles. Copper came next; several factories that produced electrical instruments had been closed. Shortage of tin meant that less food was being canned. Listening to the figures, Vaughan realized that Russia had been hit harder than the western world.

He was asked: 'Do you have proof of your contention that we are being robbed by extra-terrestrial raiders?'

'Can you give me another explanation that fits the facts? Remember, most of the thefts have been from closely guarded premises. Surely, it is unthinkable that any human agency could be at work?'

The man in the fur coat stared at Vaughan. The others talked amongst themselves.

Vaughan said: 'I have been collecting data on strange phenomena seen in the sky. Lights, saucer-shaped objects. There has been a very large number of these reports since the disappearances began. I think they refer to spaceships in which alien beings visit our planet.'

Fedora translated: 'Similar phenomena have been observed over Russia.'

There was a lull in the conversation. Vaughan became conscious that all eyes were on him, expectant. He couldn't think what they expected of him, so he produced the Dunstead photograph and passed it round.

'This picture was taken in a uranium store in the south of England, immediately prior to the disappearance of a new batch of 235. Professor Stanley, who took the photograph, also vanished. He was found later, dead, in a remote part of the countryside.'

The Russians became excited when they studied the picture.

'It is your belief, Mr. Vaughan, that this creature is one of the beings responsible for stealing our metals?'

Vaughan shrugged.

'It seems likely, in the circumstances. According to the experts at the London zoo, it is no native bat.'

'And what do you suggest we do if your theory is correct?'

'I don't know. It seems to me that the subject should be discussed at top level. After all, if I'm right, then the future of our civilization is threatened — it is a task for world governments to tackle together. Perhaps a special session of the United Nations should be called . . . '

Fedora did not translate the conversation that followed. Vaughan guessed the Russians were arguing amongst themselves; some appeared convinced. The sharp-featured man was obviously saying that the whole thing was a trick . . . only he could not explain how uranium vanished from a guarded store.

Vaughan waited anxiously. To him, it seemed that the whole world was in danger — a united effort must be obtained if the invaders from space were to be defeated.

And the Soviet Union comprised a very large part of Earth, both in men and materials. Now was no time for political squabbles.

Even if Russia agreed to co-operate, he could not see what was to be done. But there must be some way to deal with this threat. The important thing was to have the problem recognized for what it was and set the best brains throughout the world to solve it. If Earth split into factions, east and west, then the chances of survival were weakened.

Suppose the losses continued. A world without atomic power, electricity, the metals on which civilization depended. Suppose . . .

'Don't you see,' he said, voicing his thoughts aloud, 'we've just got to work together!'

Fedora translated. The Russians looked at him then to the man in the fur coat — and that huge, bear-like figure nodded its head.

'We will discuss the problem with other governments at a session of the United Nations.'

Vaughan left the Kremlin by car and was driven to the airport. He said goodbye to Fedora and boarded his plane. The two R.A.F. pilots were waiting for him.

'Mission accomplished?' one asked lightly.

Vaughan nodded, thinking that the real job was only just beginning. He looked up at the sky. Somewhere up there . . .

'Get this thing moving . . . I must see the Prime Minister immediately!'

★ ★ ★

Darkness lay like a shroud over the land. A wind blew through the treetops and ruffled the moorland ferns. It was a bleak, desolate spot that the atomics divisions of International Chemicals had chosen for its research laboratories, far from the lights of any city.

The night was moonless and a single watchman patrolled the grounds behind a high wire fence.

Far off, lights glimmered and moved through the sky. They flicked off, and, minutes later, an ovoid shape came whistling down. It landed in the wood behind the laboratories and the night became silent again.

A circular hatch opened and shadowy figures flitted out; and the small animals who inhabited that part of the wood turned tail and fled as if before a forest fire. Monstrous shadows flapped on great wings between the trees, sailing high to glide in over the wire fence.

Before the locked doors of the storeroom, they — vanished. The watchman neither saw nor heard anything. Inside the store, bars of precious metals lay in steel racks. The intruders opened no door or window, neither did they need light. They stood in a circle about the metal, silent and motionless . . . and, one by one, the bars of metal disappeared.

Time passed.

When the storeroom contained nothing that they required, the shadowy things withdrew. Outside again, they spread their wings and flapped off into the night. Darkness hid them and the wood swallowed them up. The circular hatch closed; the ship rose into the sky. Momentarily, lights showed.

The watchman continued his round, unaware that he no longer had anything of value to guard.

And high in the sky, a red flare glittered and was gone.

8

World Divided

New York basked in the warm sunshine of an Indian summer. The aircraft carrying Neil Vaughan flew down from Newfoundland, crossing the length of Long Island. As the plane glided in, he could see Manhattan's towering skyscrapers beyond the East river, tall and grey, windows glittering in the sunlight.

The plane landed, and Ann was waiting. Vaughan hadn't been sure she would be at the airport to meet him, but he had no difficulty in picking her out from the crowd. Petite, blonde and shapely, she seemed the most striking of all those waiting to greet the passengers. He had time to observe that she wore a white blouse with a black-and-grey checked skirt before she was in his arms, kissing him.

'What happened to your face, Neil?'

He still had plaster on one cheek, though he had dispensed with the head-bandage. He told her about the accident, and the man who had turned into a bat.

She was silent a moment; then —

'I've a cab waiting, Neil — you'll stay at my parents' home while you're in New York.'

She gave an address in Queens district to the driver and the cab moved off.

'It seems a long time, since London,' Ann sighed.

'Ages,' Vaughan agreed. 'I've been to Moscow since then.'

'And I've been to Bolivia!'

They compared notes, and Vaughan learnt that the United States government had sent her to South America to investigate a report of tin missing from a refinery. He showed her the photograph of the Dunstead bat.

'So that's what we're up against,' she said. 'And tomorrow there will be a special session of the United Nations Security Council. I do hope they take us seriously. I'm as convinced as you are that our planet is being plundered by aliens from another world — but can we make them see that?'

'We've got to,' Vaughan said grimly. 'This is no time for quarrelling amongst ourselves. Even if all the countries of Earth unite, I'm not sure we shall win the battle. We know so little about the raiders . . . except that they have the power to remove metals from a guarded store, leaving no trace. That argues a science superior to our own. It's going to be a tough fight — with the fate of Earth hanging in the balance.'

'I know — and politicians can be so stupid! But at least you've got the Russians willing to co-operate. I wish I could be as sure of the American delegates. One, at least, will be against any form of deal with the Soviet, on principle.'

The cab moved into Forest Hills and stopped outside a solid brownstone house on Metropolitan Avenue, Ann paid off the driver and took Vaughan's arm, leading him up a short flight of steps to the front porch. She let herself in with her own key, and called:

'I'm back, Mom, with Neil — come and meet him.'

The middle-aged lady who came smiling from the kitchen had grey in her hair and an apron over a plain cotton dress.

'Welcome, Neil,' said Mrs. Delmar. 'Ann hasn't stopped talking about you since she came back, so I feel I know you already. Make yourself at home — we don't stand on ceremony here. Ann, your father's in the library. Keith, too. You'll excuse me, Neil, I have a roast in the oven.'

The sound of jazz came from the library. Mr. Delmar was reading a newspaper while a sixteen-year-old youth was listening, enrapt, to music.

Ann said, briskly: 'Turn that noise off, Keith. Neil is here.'

The boy made a face at her, but obeyed. Mr. Delmar rose, holding out his hand in greeting.

'Sure glad to meet you, Mr. Vaughan. Any friend of my daughter's is welcome here.' He was a tall, upright man with a firm handshake. 'I hope you'll be staying a while with us.'

'I'd like to.'

'And this is Keith, my young brother,' Ann said.

The youth raised his hand in casual greeting.

'Hiya, Neil!' He wore blue jeans with a check shirt; his hair was tousled and his face freckled. 'You keen on jazz? The real old-time stuff, I mean — Dixieland?'

'I can't say I am, Keith. Music for me is Beethoven and Brahms.'

'Yeah, they're O.K., I guess, but for the hot stuff, you want Dixieland style.'

Mr. Delmar laughed.

'Neil didn't come here to discuss jazz, son. You go and get cleaned up for dinner. You'll take a glass of sherry, Mr. Vaughan?'

Dinner was served promptly; roast turkey with asparagus and French beans, apple fritters and coffee. By the end of the meal, Vaughan felt at home; they were easy-going folk, interested in the old country, and the house had a comfortable lived-in air about it.

Later, Ann whispered in his car: 'You're accepted, Neil!'

'That goes both ways — I like your family. Makes me wish . . . '

'What?' she asked promptly.

'Nothing.' Vaughan sighed. 'I can't help thinking about tomorrow — so much depends on it. Perhaps we've no future at all . . . '

Vaughan went early to bed and rose the next morning with the feeling that important events were about to take place.

Over breakfast, Ann said:

'Richard will be calling for us at nine-thirty.'

'Richard?'

'Mr. Stokes, my boss.'

Promptly at the half-hour, Stokes drove up in a long limousine. Vaughan watched from a window as he came up the steps, a distinguished man in a dark pinstripe. He pressed the bell-push and waited. Vaughan heard footsteps cross to the door, and Stokes' voice.

'Good morning, Ann. Ready to leave?'

She called Vaughan and introduced

him. Stokes' manner was polite, but chilly, and Vaughan wondered why. It seemed to him that Stokes' attitude was forced, that he was watching the two of them from the corner of his eye.

Stokes said: 'You'll be doing most of the explaining Vaughan. Ann and I will confirm your report. Let's hope we get some action.'

Stokes drove, with Ann sitting beside him and Vaughan in the back. They moved along Metropolitan Avenue to 69th Street, and swung left along Borden Avenue to the midtown tunnel. The tunnel dived beneath East River, a brightly lit concrete thoroughfare, the smell of gasoline not quite removed by an air-conditioning plant. Nose to tail, cars roared through the tunnel, the noise echoing and reverberating in the confined space. Vaughan was glad when they came out into the fresh air of Manhattan and cruised along Roosevelt Drive to the United Nations building.

Across the river, ships were unloading at the wharves while upstream, Queensboro Bridge glinted in the sun. Stokes parked before the United Nations head-quarters, a towering block of steel and glass that dominated the waterfront. They showed their passes and went inside.

Stokes said: 'This is a special session of the Security Council, and news media are being rigidly excluded. The president hopes to keep the meeting secret; personally, I doubt if that's possible. I hate to think what will happen when the public learn the subject of our talk today.'

They were conducted to a large chamber where chairs were set round a circular table. Some members of the council had already taken their places; others were coming in by twos and threes. The room began to fill up.

Already small cliques were forming, British and American. The Russian delegates sat stolidly apart. There was a low buzz of talk, an atmosphere of tension. Vaughan felt a wave of discouragement sweep over him as he looked round. This was all wrong . . .

At ten a.m., the doors of the conference room were locked, and the chairman rapped the table with his gavel.

There was an uneasy silence, into which someone coughed. The chairman rose and spoke.

'Gentlemen, some of you already have knowledge of the particular subject for discussion. For the benefit of those members whose countries are not directly involved, I will summarize events. During past months, strange things have been happening right across the world. Valuable raw materials, including uranium and copper, have disappeared . . . '

After the opening speech came a report from the British Foreign Secretary, who gave details of the Dunstead losses. He was followed by the senior American delegate who concentrated on the Fort Knox affair. A Frenchman spoke next; tin and copper were vanishing from the colonies. Delegates from China and the Far East revealed that they too had not been immune from the thefts. Then it was the turn of the Russians.

Spencer, the American delegate, stared rudely, openly antagonistic. His face conveyed the impression that he regarded all Russians as liars and blamed them for everything. The Soviet representative ignored him, speaking concisely, giving a comprehensive list of the metals missing from his country.

The Chairman turned to Vaughan.

'Mr. Vaughan,' he explained, 'was put in charge of an investigation by the British Prime Minister. He has a theory to put before you concerning these occurrences — a theory which may seem fantastic at first. Nevertheless, I beg you to give him a hearing, for if he is correct, then we face a threat greater than any the people of Earth have yet encountered.'

Vaughan spoke from notes. He told of his investigations, emphasizing the impossibility of removing uranium from Dunstead or gold from Fort Knox. He also gave a detailed report of newspaper accounts relating to mysterious things seen in the sky.

He was interrupted: 'Mr. Chairman, what has this absurd rigmarole to do with us? I protest at a waste of valuable time.'

The Chairman used his gavel to obtain silence; he had been primed in advance on the subject matter of Vaughan's speech.

'I must ask you to control your irritation at this apparent irrelevancy. This is a most important matter. Pray continue, Mr. Vaughan.'

Vaughan went on, noting the correlation of times between the disappearances and the reports of 'flying saucers.' He showed the photograph that Professor Stanley had taken, and gave the opinion of the zoo experts. Then he stated his belief, that Earth was being raided by beings from another world.

Ann Delmar gave her report and said that she agreed with Vaughan's findings. Stokes added that he had the utmost faith in Miss Delmar. The British Foreign Secretary said that his Prime Minister was inclined to take Vaughan's theory seriously. The Russian delegate indicated that his country was prepared to discuss the matter further.

Everyone seemed to be talking at once. The Bolivians were excited; the Canadians taciturn. The hubbub increased in volume and it was some minutes before the Chairman achieved a relative silence.

Spencer was on his feet. He was a lean, acid-faced man with an accusing finger and gimlet eyes.

In clipped tones, he declared: 'Let us not lose our heads gentlemen. What you have heard is too fantastic to be taken seriously. Are we to believe that giant bats bore through solid steel and concrete and remove uranium ore? That they come from Mars in a flying saucer? Really, gentlemen, such ideas are suitable only for the comic strips.'

His finger stabbed the air in front of him.

'I have little doubt that Mr. Vaughan and Miss Delmar have put forward their preposterous theory — and I repeat, theory, for they have not one atom of proof — in good faith. But they have been duped! I do not think we need look beyond this planet for the real culprits. The United States has suffered a severe blow in losing our stockpile of uranium 235; our economy is threatened by the theft from our gold reserves . . . and I ask you, who has most to gain from plundering the resources of the world? Need we look further than the Communist powers? I declare — '

The rest of his speech was drowned by the uproar that ensued.

The Chairman rapped on the table again and again, calling for silence. Vaughan groaned; he dare not look at the Russian delegates.

At last, some semblance of order was obtained — and lost immediately, for Spencer shouted:

'The alleged Soviet losses are nothing but a big bluff to put us off the scent!'

'Order, order!'

Spencer subsided, sitting stiffly in his seat and glaring at the Soviet delegates. A sudden hush followed, and the leader of the Russian party rose ponderously to his feet, a grim smile playing about the corners of his mouth.

'I repeat that my country has suffered similar losses, and, while Mr. Spencer considers us to have superhuman powers, we cannot believe that his countrymen are so clever that they can remove uranium and other metals from a closely guarded site on Soviet territory!' He paused, looking directly at Vaughan.

'My country will willingly co-operate with anyone sincerely trying to get to the bottom of this matter, whether — ' and the smile broadened — 'whether those responsible come from Mars, or some less remote place. We shall now withdraw, as a protest against the attitude of the member for the United States.'

His party rose as one man and walked out, and the Chairman adjourned the proceedings for lunch.

Vaughan felt depressed and hardly tasted his food — even the sight of Ann, across the table, did nothing to cheer him. Stokes was frankly embarrassed by his countryman's attitude.

'It might have been better to suppress that photograph,' he suggested. 'Thanks to the cinema and television, Americans are only too familiar with all manner of aliens from other planets. Giant bats are something of an anti-climax.'

'What will happen now?' Vaughan asked dejectedly.

Stokes shrugged.

'Nothing much, I imagine. The talk will simply peter out, and we'll be back where we started.'

'We've got to do *something*,' Ann said. 'Neil, you must speak again. Impress on them the danger of a world divided.'

Stokes left to go on some business of his own and Vaughan walked back to the council chamber with Ann.

'You know,' he said thoughtfully, 'Stokes is in love with you.'

Ann looked quickly at him. 'I know. He asked me to marry him — I said it was impossible.'

Vaughan didn't press the subject further.

The afternoon session began, without the Russians. Vaughan spoke again, to little avail. While the politicians about the table were completely mystified by the vanishing metals, they appeared unable to accept the idea that those responsible might come from another planet.

Vaughan was not really surprised. The exploration of the solar system, manned and unmanned, had to date given no indication of even primitive life anywhere else, much less an advanced race of beings capable of the thefts.

As Stokes had prophesied, the conference petered out with no decision being taken on any practical steps to follow.

Vaughan stayed overnight at the Delmar home, then packed his bags to fly back to London.

'The only thing I can think of,' he told Ann, 'is to place armed guards inside the store-sheds. If any bats show up, shoot them! A material corpse should go a long way to proving our point . . . and we might effectively discourage them from stealing our raw materials.'

At the airport he kissed Ann goodbye.

'We'll meet again soon,' he promised. 'Let's hope we'll have cleared up this business by then.'

His plane took off, carrying him back across the Atlantic. He wondered: what would happen now? If only Spencer had held his tongue . . . if only some definite policy to combat the invaders had been reached. But now, what chance was there, with east set against west?

He sighed, settled back in his seat.

Below him, through the clouds, the Atlantic was a deep blue-green with white crests brilliant in the sun. Strangely, his lasting memory of the trip to New York was of a brownstone house in Forest Hills, and a homely family he longed to join.

9

Crisis

The news broke with screaming headlines:

MARTIANS INVADE EARTH!

GIANT BATS STEAL URANIUM

UNITED NATIONS PLAN INTERPLANETARY WAR!

Vaughan read the newspaper accounts and listened to the tv and radio bulletins with a sense of frustrated fury. The media enjoyed a field day, boosting circulation and viewing figures by several millions. Exactly how the news had leaked out, Vaughan did not know — but, the more he read and heard, he wished that some official pronouncement had been made. Anything would be better than this . . .

At a special session of the Security

131

Council, British and American secret agents revealed the truth behind a series of daring raids that have depleted the world of valuable metallic deposits.

Giant bats from the planet Mars swoop down in their spaceships and rob secret storehouses of gold and uranium! They come in flying saucers and have incredible scientific powers, including the ability to vanish the instant they are detected.

How will Earth defend itself against the Menace from Mars?

There was much more in the same vein. It seemed to Vaughan that the reporters had gone mad. One or two papers tried to ridicule the whole affair, pointing out that the entire surface of Mars had been surveyed many times, and shown to be completely devoid of any signs of life. But proponents of the Martian theory countered by saying that Mars evidently had an underground civilization, hidden from view. As their planet had become slowly depleted of air and water over thousands of years, so the Martians had retreated underground.

Now they were casting covetous eyes on the Earth . . .

The sheer illogicality of this theory did not deter its many adherents. Who had first dreamt up the Martian angle Vaughan could not imagine, but there it was, in black and white . . .

MONSTERS FROM MARS!

It would have been ludicrous if it were not for the panic that ensued. All over the world, people read the reports and believed them. Riots broke out in Rio de Janeiro; in Mexico, the army revolted; the French cabinet resigned; in Rome, ten people were killed and over a hundred injured in street fights.

The British Prime Minister issued a denial, and, for a time, things quietened. But the damage had been done. People everywhere were uneasy.

The raids continued. Uranium, silver, tin and copper vanished. Gold disappeared from the Bank of England.

In one factory, a bat was seen — and fired at. But it disappeared before the guard's startled eyes and the bullet lodged in a wall behind.

In the days that followed, reports of flying saucers hit the headlines in a big way:

MARTIANS OVER LONDON

Last night hundreds of people in the home counties saw a procession of red and green lights move across the sky. Observers at amateur observatories say the lights came from disc-shaped objects flying at high altitude. What new outrage will be revealed as the result of this? When is the government going to take action?

Someone had only to ring a newspaper office with a story that they had seen something strange in the sky and a special edition was printed. Newspapers sold quicker than ice cream in a heatwave, and science fiction magazines trebled their circulation.

Vaughan had to give up collecting data. It seemed that every paper and journal throughout the world was giving front-page space to the invaders; daily, fresh accounts of moving lights and saucer-shaped ships came in. And he could not be sure that half of them were based on fact.

There was another scare. This time, in the United States; a television programme advertising somebody's toothpaste filled the screen with fake shots of a flying-saucer coming in to land. Right across the North American continent, viewers saw a horde of giant bats surge from a circular porthole in the ship's side, armed with fantastic weapons.

A panic ensued; three women committed suicide; fifteen people were killed and a large number injured on the roads as drivers sought to leave the danger zone. The militia were called out and the President found it necessary to make a personal broadcast, giving the lie to the invasion scare.

On Wall Street, and in the City, bankers and financiers went into a huddle. Gold was continuing to vanish from guarded vaults and, already, there was not enough bullion to cover the banknotes in circulation. As one financial paper put it:

IS OUR ECONOMY THREATENED?

Alarm has spread through the financial world at the prospect that our gold reserves are breaking down. What will happen if a group of large investors call for coverage in bullion? It is clear that any large-scale conversion is now impossible. Must we, then, create a new standard of exchange? Surely the time has come for the government to give a definite lead on world events?

But governments throughout the world maintained a bleak silence. What little they knew was confined to a small circle of intimates. Meanwhile, the newspapers printed sensational stories and the man in the street did not know what to think. It was like living in a nightmare.

At one place, two guards disappeared along with a stock of sheet tin; both were found later, dead, with every appearance of having fallen from a great height.

The thefts continued. Other metals

were added to the list; aluminium, cobalt, nickel, tungsten; industrial diamonds, too, found favour with the invaders from outer space. The steel industry ran into difficulties as the materials for various alloys became in short supply. It was impossible to keep this development from the public, for the metals were taken from industrial concerns, and one factory after another closed down through lack of raw materials.

A metal famine spread across the world . . . and powerful vested interests put pressure on the government to get something done.

This slow, steady drainage of our reserves, stated *The Times*, is undermining our whole civilization.

Unemployment figures mounted and became a serious embarrassment to the governments of many countries.

Britain's Prime Minister summoned Vaughan and Irwin to a cabinet meeting at 10 Downing Street, and it was decided that an official statement must be issued. The statement was carefully prepared, giving the facts so far as known, and imploring the country to remain calm. Everything that could be done was being done.

The R.A.F. was ordered to maintain ceaseless patrol of the night skies and force down anything resembling a 'flying saucer.' The only result of this was a number of conflicting eye-witness accounts, and the total destruction of a harmless transport plane which had lost its way in a fog and ventured too close to the Dunstead plant.

The P.M.'s statement might have been just the sheet-anchor needed to maintain stability in a world in turmoil — but for a paranoic politician with a Hitler complex. This man, Maximillian Woodroffe, had long desired power and had gathered about him a small group of neurotic followers. In normal times, he was treated as a joke, but now, with uncertainty spreading like a plague in the hearts of the people, he saw the chance to make his bid for supreme power.

He issued a manifesto calling on the government to resign, berated those in power for doing nothing while the whole

Earth was plundered of her natural resources . . . and promised a speedy end to the Martian menace if he were made dictator.

It is a measure of the degree to which wild newspaper stories had instilled panic into the public that he found so much support for his party. Woodroffe's organisation marched on Westminster and made demonstrations in Downing Street. There was fighting between the police and demonstrators. Rioting became a daily occurrence; and, in the end, the army had to be called upon to keep order in London.

Woodroffe fled abroad, but wherever he went, he found new adherents for his party. He moved from Europe to America, using every turn of events for his own advantage.

It must not be thought that governments were idle in this matter, but Woodroffe's antics, though serious, were but a pinprick compared to the major problem! There was now no doubt in the minds of those fully informed, that creatures from another world were plundering Earth's stock of raw materials;

and not content with taking the metals in their natural state, they must wait till our technicians had refined the ores and prepared them for use!

It was humiliating to admit the truth, but there seemed little that could be done to prevent the aliens taking what they wanted. The problem of exactly how they removed the stuff without leaving a trace — and rarely being seen — had still not been solved.

Industry was slowing down and would soon be helpless. Some headway had been made at switching over those products normally made of the lost metals to a plastic base. But there remained much to be done. Tinned food stocks were used up and cans were at a premium. Concentrated food tablets were issued in some of the towns hardest hit; and experiments were rushed through with other forms of container.

At 10 Downing Street, a worried Premier informed his cabinet, 'Unless some definite action is taken soon, I shall be forced to declare a state of emergency.'

Ann Delmar arrived back in London.

'In the States,' she said, 'there are now two factions — those who still believe the Soviet is responsible, and those who think we must combine forces to beat an invader from space. There is conflict in high quarters; some want all available material devoted to preparation for an all-out war against the East — others are concerned with the need to conserve what metals we have left for survival.'

London and Moscow exchanged information. Britain acted as a go-between for east and west, and the balance was delicate.

Metal stocks went down; unemployment figures soared. Woodroffe still clamoured for power. Tinned goods disappeared completely from the shops. The wheels of industry were ceasing to turn. Newspapers continued to print fantastic stories of Martians and flying saucers. The man in the street was bewildered, and politicians spent useless days and nights in discussion. Meanwhile, the creatures who looked like giant bats and came from no one knew where, went quietly about their business of removing

Earth's metals . . . Vaughan, Ann Delmar and Irwin were at Intelligence headquarters when the big news broke. Vaughan was sat reading the latest reports. Ann was on edge, her eyes ringed from lack of sleep. Irwin paced the room, muttering to himself. The telephone rang. Irwin answered it.

'Yes . . . speaking. What did you say?' He shouted his disbelief. 'Say that again!' he cried into the mouthpiece. 'Yes . . . I've got it . . . we'll be right down. Don't do anything till we get there.'

He replaced the receiver and turned to look at Vaughan and the girl. He took a deep breath. 'This is it,' he said. 'The break we've been waiting for — a flying saucer has been forced down in Surrey!'

10

Trapped

It lay in a hollow between the hills, silent and mysterious. From the point where the car stopped, Vaughan could look across the furrows of a ploughed field to the alien machine. His first reaction was one of disappointment. He thought: So this is an alien spaceship! Somehow, he had expected the first encounter to be more dramatic! The sun shone through leafless trees and gave to the earth a rich brown quality. Birds were singing, and, from a distance came the slow *phut-phut* of a farm tractor. A rabbit flopped long ears from its burrow, looked round, and dived underground again.

The quiet of the countryside was disturbed, not by the greyish metal dome in the hollow, but by military activity all around it. At a respectful distance, coils of barbed wire had been staked out to isolate the intruder; beyond the wire, groups of soldiers waited beside their guns. On the surrounding hilltops, heavy artillery covered the hollow, while three jet fighters circled hazily overhead. Sandbags had been thrown hastily about an empty barn, improvising a temporary field headquarters for the officers

A major, revolver belted at his waist and binoculars slung about his neck, stepped up to the car and saluted.

'Everything under control, Mr. Irwin,' he reported. 'The whole area is cordoned off and we are ready to meet any emergency.'

'Anything happened since it landed?'

'Nothing, sir. The machine is just where it was when I arrived with an advance unit. There has been no sign of life, no sound, nothing.'

Irwin grunted.

'All right. Let's go down and look at it close to.'

Vaughan said: 'Wait. Major, just how did the spaceship come down? Did it appear damaged? In difficulties? Exactly what happened?'

The major turned, calling: 'Henderson, just a moment, please.'

A young man in R.A.F. uniform walked across to them.

'Flight-lieutenant Henderson was the man who forced the ship down,' the major said. 'He can tell you what you want to know.'

Vaughan repeated his question.

'The whole business is quite uncanny,' Henderson began. 'I was flying at ten thousand feet, patrolling the air over Dunstead, according to orders. I had a clear sky; then high up, I saw something move. I manoeuvred into position to intercept, radioing back to base that I had spotted something.

'I can tell you I had a shock when I got a good look at it — it really looked like the pictures you see of flying saucers. Well, it came down at a hell of a lick, decelerated and circled slowly about me. I didn't like that, it was so deliberate. I was in a fine state of nerves, but I stuck to orders. I took my plane up over the ship and fired a warning burst, indicating to the pilot that he must land or I'd make things hot for him. And he landed — just like that. I was never more surprised in my life!'

'You'd say, then, that the spaceship was not damaged or otherwise out of control?'

Henderson shook his head.

'Definitely not. That thing could have accelerated and left me standing still at any time.'

Vaughan stood looking into the hollow, wondering what it meant.

Ann said: 'There's a purpose behind this. Whoever is in the ship, *wants* to meet us. There can be no other explanation.'

Vaughan nodded.

'That's how I figure it — but I'd like to know what that purpose is before we stick our necks out too far. All right, let's go down.'

Soldiers pulled back the wire for them and they walked in single file, down the slope to the spaceship, Vaughan in the lead, followed by the Major, Irwin and Ann. Cloud drifted across the sky, blotting out the sunlight. A chill spread through the hollow, leaving the ship in shadow. It became, somehow, sinister . . .

Vaughan walked round the ship, inspecting it carefully. A warning chill gnawed at his spine. A ship from space . . . from another world . . . a piece of the unknown. There were things that Man did not understand and this was one of them, dumped on his doorstep and waiting to be investigated. It was somehow frightening.

The spaceship seemed larger now that he was right up to it, an ovoid shape, fifty feet long by thirty feet wide, with a mushroom dome on top, the dome studded with circular windows at regular intervals. Its outer surface was metal, grey with a matt finish, warm to the hand. Vaughan began to wonder about the interior.

He remembered a statement by Professor Otto Brunn: 'There is no evidence whatever to support a theory of 'flying saucers' . . . the true nature of the objects seen in the sky . . . nothing more exciting than ordinary *meteorological balloons*.' He would have enjoyed seeing the professor's face if he could be confronted with this ship.

There was no visible sign of entry; the surface was smooth and unbroken. He borrowed the major's revolver and used the butt to hammer on the metal shell.

'Just to let them know we're here,' he said aloud.

They waited in a group, Ann clutching Vaughan's arm. Nothing happened.

Irwin said: 'D'you suppose it's empty?'

Vaughan started round the ship again, and exclaimed:

'Here! There's an opening . . . '

They crowded round, staring, uneasy. A circular door had slid open; beyond was darkness, an atmosphere that was warm and musky. Vaughan's nostrils twitched — the same sort of smell he had noticed at the bat enclosure in the zoo. There was no sound at all from inside, no hint of movement.

The major said, hoarsely: 'There must be someone in there — to open the door like that.'

Vaughan reversed the major's gun and pointed the muzzle into the circular opening, uncertain what to expect. The air seemed suddenly cold, the dark interior to hold a threat.

Minutes passed and still nothing happened, then Ann made up her mind.

'I'm going inside,' she said.

She did not wait, but stepped forward, into the opening. Vaughan followed her, calling back to Irwin:

'You and the major stay here — no sense in us all going into trouble. Jam the door so it can't close on us.'

Inside, he bumped into Ann, and stopped, taking her arm.

'Stand still,' she said calmly. 'It's not quite dark — let your eyes get used to it.'

There was no sound, no movement from inside the ship. Were there aliens watching them?

Irwin's voice came, anxiously: 'All right in there?'

'Yes. So far.'

Vaughan could begin to see things in a dim grey light. They were standing in a curved chamber, devoid of any furniture; the walls were smooth and unbroken, like the exterior.

Ann said: 'This must be the hold, where they store the metal.'

'In which case — '

Vaughan never finished his remark; a circular port slid silently open, inviting their inspection. He pushed forward, gun levelled. He was walking aft, and the ship tapered; beyond the portal, was another chamber, smaller, just as bare of fittings. He could not stand upright, and a solid lead wall prevented him going farther.

'Lead shielding,' Ann commented. 'This will be the power plant. I'll bet anything there's an atomic reactor behind that wall.'

There was nothing else to see so they returned to the main chamber.

'Well,' Vaughan said, looking about him, 'there's only the dome left. That must be the control room — and if there is anyone aboard, we'll find them there.'

Another door opened. Again it was circular, with no obvious mechanism; it simply slid into the wall. A sloping ramp led upwards at a steep angle, winding in a spiral about the sides of the ship. Vaughan climbed the slope, between vertical metal walls.

At the top was a third chamber, smaller

still — and just as empty. The rancid smell was stronger here and set into the walls were a number of display panels of what looked like liquid crystal. Flickering alien symbols writhed unintelligibly across their surfaces.

'Completely deserted,' Vaughan said. 'It's uncanny — the pilot *must* be somewhere.'

'Or the ship is flown by remote control,' Ann suggested. 'Perhaps we unknowingly operated some mechanism to open the doors for us.'

Vaughan frowned.

"Then there would be no need for instruments — and this smell indicates that something has been here, not very long ago. You don't suppose — ' He paused, looking round uneasily.

'Yes?' Ann prompted.

'Could they be — *invisible?*'

'Oh . . . '

They stood silently before the shining dials, wondering if invisible eyes were on them, watching their every move.

Ann said: 'A camera would hardly record an invisible animal. No, I don't think that's the answer.'

Vaughan walked slowly round the chamber, inspecting the walls, the floor, the ceiling, taking care not to touch anything.

'There are so many odd things,' he commented. 'The ship is presumably propelled by some kind of rocket action — yet we saw no vents in the exterior surface. And here, though there are recording instruments, there doesn't appear to be any form of manual control. If it were a rocket designed by Earthmen it would be full of gadgets . . . here, there is empty space.'

'We are looking at the result of an alien science, Neil; there's no reason why it should look like something designed on Earth. I've no doubt that if we knew the fundamentals of their science, everything would seem very ordinary.'

They walked down the ramp to the hold and the outside door, where Irwin and the major waited. A heavy tree stump had been dragged up and now rested half-in, half-out, of the ship, effectively preventing the door from closing.

'The ship is empty,' Vaughan said briefly, and gave an outline of what they had seen.

'Well,' said the major, 'Henderson is sure the ship was piloted — he swears that nothing could manoeuvre the way this machine did, under remote control. That means the pilot slipped away before we got here. I must have the countryside searched at once.'

The major hurried off to organize search parties.

'Well, what now?' Irwin asked. 'We've got the ship — what do we do with it?'

'Hang on to it!' Vaughan said grimly. 'I'm staying here till you can get some experts down and take it to pieces to find out what makes it tick.'

Irwin looked startled.

'Stay aboard! Are you sure that's wise? I mean the thing is *alien* . . . we don't quite know what to expect.'

'Neil is right,' Ann said. 'We'll stay together. After all, nothing very much can happen with the ship surrounded. And the secrets of the bat people are right here — we've got to dig them out.'

'All right, have it your own way.' Irwin was still reluctant. 'I'll get some scientists down immediately, and we'll see what they have to say. Sit tight.'

He started back up the slope, leaving Vaughan and Ann inside the spaceship. The silence was uncanny. Cloud obscured the sunlight and cold shadow lay across the land outside the ship. Irwin became a small figure trudging up the hill towards a group of officers. The bare limbs of trees and the precise barrels of guns made a silhouette against the sky. Beyond the wire, soldiers were setting off in parties to search for the missing pilot.

'Well,' Vaughan said, 'he — or it — won't get back to the ship without being spotted. And we'll be waiting.'

He realized that he was still holding the major's revolver, and felt foolish — there was nothing to shoot at. He slipped the gun in his pocket.

Ann said suddenly: 'The door leading aft has closed!'

Vaughan turned, crossing the chamber to the wall where the door had been. He felt the metal with his hands; it was

154

smooth as glass, with not a break in its surface. He could not be sure of the exact location of the gliding panel, so smooth was the join . . .

He looked round, quickly. The door opening on to the ramp that led up to the control room had also disappeared.

'Well, at least, the outside door — '

His voice dropped. One second, he could see the heavy tree stump sprawled across the opening, the countryside beyond; the next . . . nothing! The tree vanished as if it had never existed, and the circular port slid shut, blocking out all light.

Ann gave a cry of alarm and Vaughan darted forward, feeling for the outside wall in pitch darkness. His fingers slid uselessly over a smooth surface; there was no break, nothing to grasp. He brought out his gun and hammered at the wall. He reversed it, fired once; the slug skidded off and left no mark that he could feel.

Ann, moving round the wall with one arm outstretched, bumped into him. Her breath came quicker, and there was a nervousness in her voice.

'It seems we walked into a trap, Neil.'

'We'll get out,' he said, without the slightest conviction.

He made a full circle of the chamber, using his sense of touch to guide him, reaching Ann again without discovering any break in the smoothly curving wall. If only it wasn't so dark, if only he could see . . .

Ann whispered: 'I'm scared, Neil. The pilot must have come back; or been here all the time — we're prisoners!'

Vaughan took her in his arms to comfort her.

'Irwin will find a way to get us out.'

With the door closed and the chamber in darkness it seemed warmer, the rancid odour stronger. Vaughan was acutely aware of the thumping of his heart, a quickened beat in the stillness, measuring out the seconds.

A tremor ran through the metal floor.

Ann gasped: 'We're taking off!'

The vibration increased; somewhere, power was being poured through the ship. He thought: this is the purpose for which the ship landed — to capture specimens of the human race. Now they are taking us . . . where?

His body felt heavier, as if something pressed his feet hard against the floor. Automatically, he braced his legs.

'We're rising,' he said. 'I hope the major doesn't open up with his big guns.'

The pressure increased. 'We'd better lie down,' he decided. 'There's no telling what acceleration a ship like this is capable of.'

They stretched out on the floor. Vaughan held Ann with his left hand; his right gripped the major's revolver. The metal floor was hard and warm, vibrating in a manner that set his teeth on edge.

He began to sweat. His limbs became too heavy to move and the back of his head, forced against the floor, ached. His mouth sagged open and it became difficult to breathe. The pressure built up . . .

He was blacking out. Consciousness slid into a deep recess. He heard Ann moaning but could do nothing for her.

His stomach felt as if an elephant were treading on it and his head went round and round, expanding like a balloon. Then, pinned to the floor, he lost all awareness . . .

11

Moon Base

The period of blackout due to acceleration did not last many minutes. Vaughan opened his eyes to a majestic brilliance that dazzled and forced him to turn his head from the glare, blinking.

He sat up, abruptly aware of the alien scent, the vibration of metal walls, Ann lying still beside him. He was aboard a ship in space . . .

The knowledge engulfed him. Outer space lay beyond the hull of the ship, infinite and compelling. The wonder of it held him motionless, fascinated.

Ann stirred, struggling back to consciousness. He helped her to stand, and, for minutes, neither of them spoke, overwhelmed by what they saw.

Metal panels had slid back, revealing windows, and beyond, space was black as midnight and strewn with jewels, the stars that made up the Milky Way. Earth was a monstrous sphere, hanging suspended in emptiness and the sun a terrible incandescence, flaming-wild. The moon, startlingly large, shining brilliantly with craters and rills clearly visible, loomed ahead . . .

'I'm dreaming it,' Ann said softly.

Vaughan shook himself. The full implication of their position burst upon him like a nightmare. They were prisoners, aboard a ship leaving Earth for some unknown destination, powerless in the hands of the inhabitants of another planet. That they might ever return to Earth and pick up the thread of their lives again seemed remote in the extreme. No human being had ever before faced such a problem.

He looked quickly at Ann to see how she was taking it. Her amber eyes were dreamy as she stared at the beauties of space; she had yet to grasp the reality.

Something was missing. Vaughan had that feeling at the back of his mind, but he could not find the detail that eluded him. He prowled about the chamber, looking for something he could not define. The walls were smooth metal and glass; no door offered itself. There was nothing to sit on. The floor, bare and metallic . . .

Of course! The major's revolver — it had gone. It had been in his hand when he blacked out and now it was nowhere to be seen. He checked his pockets, looked at Ann, stared wildly about the room. He remembered firing one shot and searched for the spent bullet. That, too, had disappeared.

Vaughan had to think. The gun had gone, so that meant the ship was piloted; whoever was in charge had removed the weapon while he and Ann had been unconscious. Were they, even now, under observation?

The ship was still accelerating, slowly and smoothly, or there would have been a feeling of weightlessness. With atomic energy they had a vast power resource. It was not a limitless source of energy — as witness their interplanetary raids to replenish supplies — but, Vaughan thought, they could afford to accelerate to

161

a halfway point, then immediately start to decelerate, and the journey would take appreciably less time than otherwise.

Ann turned and looked at him thoughtfully.

'I'm glad,' she said, 'that we're together, Neil.'

He went over and put his arm about her.

'Don't be frightened, Ann.'

'I couldn't be frightened,' she answered. 'It's too wonderful for that . . . this is something I've often thought about. And now it's actually happening!'

There was a dreamlike quality in her voice.

'I wonder where they are taking us? To their own planet? Mars? Venus, perhaps? Or even beyond. And the things we'll see . . . and we'll share it all together.'

Vaughan forced a smile. He too felt something of that inner excitement she felt, but his own reaction was tempered by the question; would they ever see Earth again?

Somewhere above them, in the control dome, was the pilot. Vaughan wondered about him — or her — or *it*. There was a mystery here he could not fathom. If the pilot had been aboard the spaceship when first they searched it, why had they not seen him? And that tree trunk jamming the outer door — how had that vanished so completely? It all tied in, he supposed, with the disappearing metals . . . but how did they do it?

Beyond the window, the ball that was the planet Earth visibly dwindled in size. Vaughan remembered the men who had fallen from the sky, and shuddered. Their bodies had been recognizable, so could not have dropped from more than a few hundred feet. Surely then, the invaders had not brought Ann and him this far simply to kill them?

He turned again to Ann.

'I can't wait any longer. This may be the end for us. Whatever happens now it's outside our control — death may come suddenly, and I want you to know that I love you, and had intended to ask you to marry me, but now . . . '

She clung to him.

'I wouldn't change anything,' she

whispered. 'Whatever happens, we'll be together.'

The hours passed. Earth was a pale disc, featureless, in the black void, with incredibly distant stars studded about like random gems. The sun blazed, lighting the ship with harsh brilliance — and Vaughan was glad of the light. It showed that the compartment was empty, with nothing to fear.

He dreaded that darkness might come again, swiftly, leaving them to imagine what might follow.

There were material problems to engage his mind. Hunger. They did not need food immediately but sooner or later, they must find something to eat. And where, in that strangely empty ship? Water was more important. Whenever he thought of water, thirst assailed him. They could not go long without water . . .

Did the raiders intend to care for them? Or were they to be left to die, slowly, and in agony. Vaughan could not make up his mind about the real purpose behind their abduction; and all depended on that.

Another mystery was the air in the

room. While he did not feel certain that its composition corresponded exactly with the atmosphere of Earth, it was similar enough for them to breathe without difficulty. Did that mean the aliens came from a similar world? Or had the atmosphere of the chamber been specially adapted for them?

But the thing that really worried him was the problem of communication. Some time, he supposed they would come face to face with the pilot, or others of his kind — and how were they to understand each other? That these mysterious beings would talk English was an idea too fantastic to take seriously. He remembered his difficulties in Moscow. How much harder it would be to talk to creatures who probably had no knowledge of any language on Earth!

Ann, tired of standing, was sitting on the metal floor, her back against the gently curving wall. She still watched the universe beyond the windows, fascinated.

Vaughan envied her detachment from the fears that oppressed him. Her pleasure had the naivety of a child.

She became aware that he watched her, and turned her head, smiling.

'It's the moon, Neil. They are taking us to the moon!'

Vaughan studied the view through the windows.

Earth seemed incredibly remote and the moon hung large before them. The sunlit side was a brilliant white, marked with dark chasms and craters; the shadow side faintly illumed by Earthlight. It grew larger and he could not doubt that she was right. The ship was heading directly for the moon.

But why? It was a dead world, airless, without water, incapable of supporting life. Surely the raiders could not have originated there?

Acceleration stopped. There was a moment of weightlessness. Instinctively, Vaughan started towards Ann, but he was helpless to control his movements.

Touching the wall with his hand, he sailed up and away, floating through air. His head hit the ceiling and he rebounded, slowly, drifting floorwards. Ann, lying motionless, laughed at his antics to regain balance.

Vaughan cursed, wishing for a handrail, a rope, anything to which he could cling. The absence of gravity, while not dangerous, was certainly irritating.

It did not last long. The spaceship coasted, then deceleration commenced. Pressure built up again; Vaughan came unsteadily to the floor and stretched out, wondering if blackout would come again. But the energy required to land on the moon was less than that needed to break free from Earth's gravity. The ship decelerated steadily.

Time passed . . .

The luminous curved edge of the moon showed clear against the blackness of space, filling all the windows, a horizon broken only by jagged rock walls, high cliffs and craters many miles wide. Something flashed in the void, metal glinting in the sun.

Ann said: 'A meteor!'

It came slanting down from the dark infinities of space, attracted by the pull of the moon's gravity. Down and down it fell, with no atmosphere to impede it. For a moment it showed blackly against the glittering pumice dust; then it crashed, burrowing, breaking up . . . and another small crater was formed on the lunar surface.

The spaceship continued its elliptical course, losing speed and height. Below lay a great walled plain; a long rift in the bleak landscape, straight and narrow the dazzle of sunlight reflected by rock crystals; intense black shadows thrown by a high mountain chain. Desolation.

'We're going round to the other side,' Ann said. 'The other side of the moon!'

Vaughan tensed. In circling the Earth Luna always kept one face averted. But he knew that the back of the moon had been photographed and scanned by space probes — even seen at first hand by orbiting astronauts. Surely it was not possible that the aliens originated from there?

The ship rushed nearer. Earth was a pale disc, close to the horizon, four times as large as the moon appears to us sinking slowly to disappear from view. Vaughan stared interestedly at the moonscape

— and was perplexed.

Perhaps Columbus was disappointed when he discovered America. All that Vaughan saw was a continuation of the previous scene; a desert of fine rock dust, slate, lava, dark crags. There were more craters, some with a central peak, some without, and a long broken line of mountains. No vegetation, no hint that life might exist anywhere on that barren satellite.

'Why have we come here?' Vaughan spoke his thoughts aloud. For there was no longer room to doubt that the ship was going to land. It swooped lower with every second and an enormous crater, a hundred miles across, loomed into view.

'They may live below ground,' Ann said.

The stark emptiness of the lunar landscape was impressive, frightening, incredible. A world without air, so there could be no sound. No winds — so no weather as it was known on Earth. The sky was unrelieved blackness, the sun's corona fully revealed. No rivers or rainfall, no trees or grass; just rocks, subjected alternately to intense heat and freezing cold as the moon turned on its axis. Under such conditions, mountains would crack and crumble, erode away, leaving plains of fine dust. A world of bleached dust and jagged rock — and silence.

The spaceship was dropping towards the crater. Vaughan glimpsed towering walls, a shallow bowl — and something else. Two sections of the crater floor seemed to be moving apart. A dark crack appeared in the heart of the crater. Now exposed, something glittered — a dome of misty glass. And under it . . . he could not be certain, but he thought he detected movement.

Lower the ship sank, and, abruptly, metal panels slid across the windows and they were in total darkness again. Ann clutched at Vaughan's arm. The vibration of the floor lessened and the pressure due to deceleration eased. He waited for the shock of landing, braced himself for the impact.

Every second dragged. They had no way of telling what was happening. The darkness was hot, smelly, like the folds of an old blanket, stifling them.

It came suddenly, after he had given up expecting it. A rocking motion, gentle, soothing, as the spaceship settled to rest.

Ann said, a hysterical note in her voice: 'We've landed on the moon!'

There was nothing to do but wait. Someone — or something — would come for them; meanwhile there was utter silence. Not a sound came from the ship or outside. Vaughan stood with his arms about the girl; her body was taut and he could sense the quickening beat of her heart. The darkness bred fear . . .

Metal panels slid back and light streamed in through the windows. Outside —

'The door,' Ann whispered urgently. 'It's opening!'

Vaughan turned to the circular opening that concealed the ramp leading up to the control room; and saw for the first time, the pilot of their ship.

12

Alien Intelligence

Vaughan stared, without surprise. Indeed, at that moment, he was not conscious of any feeling at all. Everything was curiously unreal, the view from the window, the hot and smelly chamber, the dull metal walls. It was as if he stood outside himself, detached, and observed . . .

He thought: just like the photograph Stanley took. The pilot was so exactly like the bat in the Dunstead picture that Vaughan imagined he could easily be the same one.

He stood in the doorway, wings folded about him, grey fur smooth and silky. Bright, intelligent eyes looked out from a sharply pointed head; the feet, Vaughan noted, were sufficiently developed to carry his weight. There were no hands — as we know them — for the fingers had become part of the wing structure, but the thumbs extended free.

The wings were formed from a thin membrane and joined the neck to the ankles and stub of a tail. The legs were short, the head squat; he seemed all body and wings.

Vaughan and the pilot remained motionless, each taking the other's measure; then Ann's voice broke the strained silence:

'I'm scared, Neil!'

Yes, Vaughan thought grimly, these things were nightmare creatures . . .

The pilot moved forward, brushing past Vaughan to disappear through the outer door, which opened automatically for him in some mysterious way. Vaughan was reminded of the white rabbit in Alice; the bat had the same preoccupied manner. It was irritating; surely they were not going to be completely ignored after being brought to the moon?

The alien stopped outside the ship and looked back.

Ann said: 'I imagine we're meant to follow.'

Vaughan became aware that he was breathing air from outside the ship. It was warm, humid, tainted by a rancid odour; but undeniably an atmosphere related in kind to that of Earth.

He stepped outside, stumbled, and staggered forward. His body felt curiously light and it was some minutes before he mastered the art of walking in the moon's lesser gravity. Ann followed him carefully, putting her feet down as if she moved on a sheet of ice.

A crowd of bat-people gathered to watch their antics, twittering amongst themselves. The noise was like the chatter of birds rising and falling; a continuous stream of meaningless sound. Vaughan knew then that they were never going to be able to talk to their captors.

He stood still, looking about him. High above, an opaque dome sealed in the atmosphere; he wondered about that — it must be a remarkable material to withstand the temperature variation. There would be an airlock too, he supposed, for the ships to come inside, but he could not see it. Water lay in a pool scooped out of the rock. All about him, the close-pressed ranks of bats surged. At first they all looked alike, but as he studied them, he began to see individual differences. Some were larger than others, there was a variation of texture and colour in the fur, some male, others female — one at least was pregnant — while some babies tumbled at play. He noticed that the older males had long, fine whiskers, and that the females were generally larger than the males.

They chattered ceaselessly, making small squeals and grunts, chirping, twittering.

Ann commented: 'I guess they've never seen anything like us before — I feel like an exhibit at a side-show!'

But the bats soon tired of the spectacle; in ones and twos they spread their wings and flew off; leaving only the pilot of the ship with Vaughan and the girl. The ground was hard and smooth as concrete; rock-dust which had been treated in a special way. And there were spaceships, lined up in groups of seven, row upon row. Vaughan judged that there must be nearly a hundred ships in all, and some of them were huge.

It staggered him to see those ships — no wonder there had been so many newspaper reports! But it was the large ships that really caught his eye. They must have been all of five hundred feet long, ovoid, and of the same grey metal with a dome on top.

Ann gripped Vaughan's arm, pointing upwards.

'Another ship coming in, Neil.'

They watched. Outside the murky glass, a dark shape hung suspended. A circular port opened and the ship moved. A pause. Then another opening, the ship moving through and down, landing as gently as a bubble floats through air.

'They must have constructed two domes,' Vaughan conjectured, 'one inside the other. The gap between acts as an airlock.'

A single bat left the ship when it landed . . . and then Vaughan saw the most incredible sight of all.

Scores of the aliens surrounded the ship in a circle. They stood on the ground, unmoving, almost as if they were asleep — and, suddenly, *bars of metal began to form on the ground in front of the ship*. It was impossible, but it happened. Vaughan rubbed his eyes. Not one of the bats had moved, yet the stack of metal rose higher with every second. The bars just seemed to materialize from nowhere. It was Ann who put his turbulent thoughts into words.

'Neil, don't you see, they're unloading the ship! This is another batch of metal stolen from Earth.'

Vaughan struggled to accept the idea.

'But how do they do it?'

She had no answer. The strange spectacle continued until the ship was empty; by that time, a large pile of metal bars stood on the ground. Then the circle of giant bats came to life — they flew off, as if the metal had no further interest for them.

Ann walked across to a tunnel sloping into the ground. It was dark inside, but she saw the opening of a cave; and, hanging from the roof, were hundreds of man-sized bats — upside down, wings folded, bright eyes gleaming. It was a frightening sight and she backed out quickly.

Vaughan commented: 'They seem at home either way up — it must be a big advantage in a ship in space.'

The pilot of the ship that had brought them followed them around but he made no attempt at communication and seemed content simply to keep them in view.

'They seem very sure that we're harmless,' Vaughan said. 'I don't like it — I wish we could shake their confounded superiority!'

He was impressed by the colony. In this crater on the moon the bat-people had created a world all their own; and it was completely artificial; the dome, its atmosphere, the water supply — nothing belonged. Everything had been created for the aliens' existence here.

And they'd chosen a crater on the side that never faced Earth: that, he felt sure, was deliberate. No Earth-based or satellite telescopes could reveal this alien colony so close to the mother planet, yet so surely hidden. The entrance to their underworld was covered by a natural crater, so even if orbiting probe cameras from Earth had photographed it, they would not have seen anything untoward. It would only become revealed when the alien ships were arriving or leaving, and they had taken good care not to be observed at such times. He wondered how long they had been established here; probably quite recently — and at a time when Earth had no current programme of lunar exploration or observation.

Farther on, beyond the large spaceship, was a dome of grey metal, some thirty feet high. As they approached a circular door opened.

Ann said: 'They don't mind what we see, apparently. I should judge this to be the powerhouse.'

It was — and more. Inside, screened by a lead shield was the atomic pile. Vaughan guessed that the flickering displays were registering the level of energy, but he saw no recognizable controls. Beside it stood what he took to be an air plant; next to that, banks of heaters. The whole assembly had the compactness of a perfect engineering job.

Outside again, around one of the large ships, new activity was taking place. A circle of bats formed; and a consignment of tinplate slowly vanished from the ground. Their guide went aboard the ship, looking back at them. Vaughan and Ann followed him

Immediately inside was the storeroom, now filled with tinplate, and Vaughan had no doubt that they had just watched the loading operation.

'They've certainly overcome the problem of manual labour,' Ann said thoughtfully, 'but exactly *how* they do it is something that baffles me completely.'

Aft was the power drive; a ramp led up to the control room, more spacious than on the ship that had brought them to the moon. Another difference was the living quarters; these large ships were equipped to carry several families. The only 'furniture' appeared to be a network of metal rods suspended from the ceiling.

Vaughan looked at Ann, and asked: 'D'you know what this means? They don't originate here at all! This colony is simply a transit camp — the smaller ships raid Earth and bring the metals here to be loaded on the big ships. Then they take the stuff — home . . . wherever that is!'

Ann nodded thoughtfully.

'It must be a very long way. Another star system. The size of the power plant, the way the ship is equipped, proves that. Imagine a spaceship with atomic energy, under constant acceleration. Such a vessel could attain near-light speed, which means they could reach nearer stellar systems in less than a dozen years or so . . . what infinite distances they can cover!

Which means, Vaughan thought grimly, that Earth's resources are gone for good! We can never bring back metals from across an interstellar gulf.

They went outside. Vaughan looked at the pilot and said, hopelessly: 'We're hungry. We need food and something to drink. He mimed the actions of eating and drinking.

The bat blinked at them, but gave no sign that he understood. Then, miraculously, four metal bowls appeared on the ground before them; two contained water, two a greenish-brown pulp.

Ann drawled: 'Quick service! I wonder if we dare . . . ?'

Vaughan squatted on the ground and picked up a bowl of water.

'It's risk it, or die of thirst. We've really no choice.'

He sipped the water, rolling it round his tongue before swallowing. It tasted brackish. He drank half the bowl and waited, half expecting dire results.

'Seems all right,' he grunted

Ann drank too, then tasted the food. It was an unpleasant-looking mess, a pulp of vegetation, Vaughan guessed. He ate hungrily. Ann finished first and licked her lips.

'I've tasted better,' she acknowledged, 'But nothing ever went down so well. It's only now that I realize how long it is since we ate. I wonder where they get their water supply?'

Vaughan wondered too; certainly there was no moisture on the moon. It must have been brought from somewhere. From Earth?

The bat moved off again, and Vaughan followed with Ann. They came to a cave, dark and gloomy, and their guide spread his wings and sailed up to the roof, to hang suspended there.

Vaughan stared at him, curious as to what was to happen now. Ann sat on the hard rock floor.

'Well, we've toured the colony,' she said. 'I imagine we're to be interviewed by someone in authority — then perhaps we'll learn the reason for our being brought here. I don't think it was just to inspect the premises.'

Vaughan sat beside her and waited. Shadows moved eerily through the cave and the air was foul with the alien stench. Beady eyes watched them from above; glittering, unwinking eyes that held the quality of intelligence unrestrained by any mercy.

Vaughan shivered; and tried to imagine what communication was possible between Earthmen and these creatures. Certainly, the food had arrived promptly — and he suspected that was not entirely due to his attempt at mime. There was something else involved, something he did not understand. Speech was out of the question and, so far, he had seen no indication that the bat-people used a written language. The markings on the indicator dials aboard the spaceship, and in the powerhouse, were simple in the extreme — probably only symbols used to differentiate one energy level from another. What —

Ann gave a startled cry and clung to him as a giant bat glided down to land beside them. Vaughan estimated that he stood eight feet high, with an extended wingspan of more than twenty-five feet. The bat was old and wrinkled and smelled as though he were in the last stage of decomposition.

Ann whispered: 'The head-man!' and Vaughan knew she was right. They were in the presence of one of the elders. The bat folded his wings about him and stood erect on the ground facing them, his bright eyes peering intently into their faces.

Vaughan waited breathlessly. Their eyes met . . . and Vaughan's consciousness

184

began to reel dizzily. Those bead-like eyes knew so much, had seen so many wonders, experienced so many worlds. They knew the universe and all it contained.

He sat and stared into the bat's gleaming eyes and it seemed he dare not shift his gaze. A paralysis spread through his limbs. Hypnotism?

His head ached. The scene began to shift, the moon-cave blurring. Something strange happened inside his brain . . . and Ann's words came from far off:

'Neil — I've a picture in my head!'

13

Ultimatum

'Telepathy!'

Vaughan was not conscious of speaking aloud; the word was torn from his lips by the sudden realization of what was taking place. But it was more than telepathy; the mode of communication was more complex than the simple impress of a thought by one mind on another.

A picture formed in the head, a mental image, with colour, scent and sound. It was almost like being transferred to another world ... and the picture Vaughan saw was another world.

A bright blue sky hung over him, brightly, blindingly blue. There was a riot of vivid greens of the vegetation, dazzling scarlets for flowers — and bats, millions of them, it seemed, filling the air with the thunder of their wings. He saw buildings and spaceships and other constructions.

It was hot, much hotter than Earth, and the rich atmosphere was heavy with alien scents.

The picture changed. He was in space, in the dark places between worlds, with the stars bright about him. He felt he should recognize the constellations, but their precise identity eluded him, and he was left with the impression that these stars would be visible through telescopes on Earth.

The scene changed again. He was swooping down between the stars, approaching a planet that circled a sun similar to Earth's own. The planet might have been Earth, but he knew it wasn't, for the star had only this one satellite. He was moving above the surface; below lay steaming jungle, swamps and immense trees. Creatures moved about the jungle — bats.

This was the home of the bat-people, millions of years in the past. He watched history in the making. There were other creatures, like those now extinct on Earth; some half-fish, half-animal; and monkeys. At this time, the bats were no larger than those of Earth — they had yet to evolve in size. Centuries passed; and he watched the struggle for survival turn into a battle for supremacy of race.

Vaughan found himself wondering what quirk of fate decided that Man should rise to be ruler of Earth, and the bats on this strangely similar world. He tried to imagine Earth if some other species had risen to power instead of Man . . .

As generation followed generation, it became obvious that the bats were destined to rule this particular world. Other life forms died out or were subjugated. Vaughan looked for the monkey tribes — surely they would develop? But no; the spark of intelligence that had raised Man above all other animals was lacking here. It was the giant bats who became the masters.

Later, he saw the planet stripped of ores for machines. Atomic power arrived; and spaceflight. Then developed a period of colonization; the bats overflowed to other worlds that could support them, and, all the time, they were going farther afield to plunder worlds for the metals they needed.

An interstellar empire sprang up; metals poured into the home planet and were converted into more ships, more machinery.

The bats rarely relaxed — always there was a restlessness that drove them on from star to star.

The bat-people knew two stages of life; childhood and maturity. There seemed no intermediate point. When they were young, they sported and enjoyed a carefree life, provided for ungrudgingly by the parents. Then, overnight, it seemed, the change occurred.

One day they circled and glided, chasing each other; the next, they worked; with no thought but to build spaceships and machines. There was no purpose that Vaughan could see, just a driving urge to create something more. Man, he supposed, must look like that to other animals.

The point of change came when the young bats developed telepathic powers. The talent was a latent one, coming with maturity; and when it came, the young bat was instantly in contact with the race mind. He stopped being an individual and became a member of the race; and it was this sudden revelation that drove him on, blindly, selflessly.

Their minds were born in that moment; from being animals content merely to exist, they became imbued with purpose. Where before, only a few thought-tracks were open in their brains, now it seemed that new channels flowered, bringing incredible talents of the mind,

Beside the ability to communicate directly in mental pictures, they had an innate control over matter. With thought alone, they were able to move objects, transmit them from one place to another — and it was this power which gave them an advantage over all other animal creations with whom they came into contact.

Vaughan was stunned by the sudden realization of what had happened on Earth. The bats teleported uranium, or gold, or anything else they wanted, from storeroom to spaceship; they were able to transmit themselves through solid walls. Thought knew no barrier.

Professor Stanley had been teleported into the air, and control relaxed; he fell to his death. The bar of silver that had fallen must have been an accident, for it transpired that teleportation had strict physical limitations. The bat-people could only operate their thought-control over short distances; which was the reason why they needed spaceships.

Their ships and machinery appeared to be without controls because the mechanism was built-in, and operated by thought-waves. Vaughan's head reeled as explanations fell into place. A bat could vanish simply by 'thinking' himself elsewhere. The pilot of the ship which had brought them to the moon had never been seen because he teleported himself from room to room — anywhere, in fact, where Vaughan and Ann were not!

And now the vanguard of the giant bats' empire had readied Earth. They needed metals, so they took them.

Uranium to fuel their power piles, metals to build new ships. There appeared to be nothing inherently vicious in the bats' nature, despite their looks; they were simply concerned with meeting their own needs, and considered other forms of life to be of no importance. What they wanted, they took . . . and their power of mind meant that none could stand against them.

Earth was about to be conquered without a gun being fired.

Sweat ran down Vaughan's face. Mankind humiliated by giant bats, beaten without a chance to fight back! But what could men do against beings with such powers? Nothing . . . nothing at all.

New images formed in his mind. The elder bat had not finished.

The problem of water was solved. They brought it from the asteroids in their ships; huge chunks of ice, floating in space, captured by teleportation and brought to the moon to be melted down.

It was made clear that the bat-people would allow nothing to stop their plans for denuding Earth of her metal deposits.

They had preferred not to come into the open; but now that their raids had been discovered, secrecy was no longer possible — and so the peoples of Earth must be made to understand that they were no longer the masters of their planet. This was the purpose for which Vaughan and Ann had been brought to the moon. They would be returned . . . to announce an ultimatum.

Work — or be exterminated!

Work for the bats! Mine ores to be handed over to the inhabitants of another world. Earth was to be turned into a slave colony, no longer to have a say in her destiny. The bat-folk were the masters now . . .

A demonstration of power would be made to bring the peoples of Earth to heel. A city would be atomized. *Paris*. The beautiful Paris, city of romance and culture and the laughter of Spring. Paris, the city that had withstood one invader after another, was to be annihilated to prove to the world that bat law must be obeyed. A hydrogen bomb would be teleported to the heart of the city, and detonated — a bomb taken from one of Earth's stockpiles.

That was the ultimatum, and a ship was ready to return Vaughan and Ann to Earth, to deliver the fatal message.

The mental contact was broken and Vaughan again became conscious of his surroundings. The cave, the vast dome overhead . . . he had to remind himself that he was on the moon.

The elder bat spread his wings, flew upwards and disappeared from view. Vaughan looked at Ann. The girl's face was white. He held her hand, pressed it, but could think of no words adequate to the situation.

High in the cave, bats hung head down, watching them; it was not their world that was coming to an end. The pilot waited. Vaughan rose and, leading Ann by the hand, walked back to the ship.

They went aboard, and the pilot disappeared up the ramp leading to the control dome. The doors closed.

Vaughan stood by a window, looking out over the colony. It was the last time he would see it; the crater and the ranks of spaceships drawn up and ready for flight.

Metal panels slid noiselessly over the windows, leaving the chamber in darkness. Vaughan and Ann lay on the floor for the take-off. Metal vibrated. A giant hand, it seemed, forced them against the floor — the ship rose, passed through the airlock, into space.

After some minutes, the pressure eased and the windows opened again. Looking back, Vaughan saw the opening sliding together in the crater; the crater dwindled behind them becoming smaller as the ship rose higher. Even that huge crater became insignificant with time. The full disc of the moon showed, half brightly lit, half in shadow, with chasms and craters gashing an airless surface.

A dead world . . . but the menace it held was only too real.

Ann sighed, turning from the window. 'All the beauty has gone out of it,' she said slowly. 'I'll never again look at the stars and feel safe.'

'We'll fight back,' Vaughan said. 'There must be a way — we'll find it, somehow.'

She shuddered.

'If only we've time to evacuate the city — '

She was thinking of Paris, and more than three million inhabitants who lived in the shadow of sudden death.

'It's . . . ' Ann searched for the right word. 'It's inhuman!'

But they're not human, Vaughan thought; we can't expect them to feel as we do. They had different standards — or were they so different, after all? Had Man ever hesitated to exterminate those who stood in his path? And wasn't the hydrogen bomb to be used on Paris going to be taken from a military store on Earth? He found it faintly ironical that Earth's most devastating weapon, designed for war amongst the nations of Earth, was to be turned loose on the whole world. Irwin might have said that the bat-people had a sense of humour, but Vaughan knew it was simply a matter of expediency.

The ship moved through an arc. The old, familiar face of the moon showed itself; and Earth made a glittering disc amongst the stars. Space was black, and no longer wonderful. It was black and threatening. What other terrors might lie out there among the stars?

Vaughan felt small and insignificant. Perhaps this was the end of mankind. Would anyone worry over that? Amongst so many worlds, would the destruction of one form of life be even noticed? He could not feel sure.

Ann said, abruptly: 'They'll believe us — after Paris . . .'

Had the bats any material weapons at all? The pen was mightier than the sword . . . and now it seemed that the power of mind was greater than any military armament. It was going to be difficult to make governments believe the facts; until Paris vanished in a holocaust.

Vaughan sighed. No two people could ever have been as unpopular as he and Ann would be when they delivered the ultimatum from the moon.

New thoughts flashed through his head. Suppose they could not find a way to defeat the invaders? He tried to imagine Earth after they had gone — an

Earth stripped bare of metallic deposits. What would life be like then? His imagination baulked at the problem he posed . . .

The hours passed. The moon receded and Earth grew in size, filling the windows with its monstrous bulk. Continents showed, oceans took on a familiar shape. In a little while they would land with their news and the desperate battle for supremacy would begin.

Vaughan wondered what had happened during their absence. The bats would not have been idle; more stocks would have disappeared. Had Russia and the United States joined forces, or were they still bickering amongst themselves? Unity was essential now . . .

How, indeed, could the invaders be beaten? Teleportation was something strange and unknown, a weapon of terrible power, and he could think of no way in which it might be countered. But they would fight; somehow the peoples of Earth would strike back at the invaders. History was one long record of the fight for freedom —

Ann slipped her hand into his, gazing into his face with a faint smile.

'You look as if all the troubles in the world rested on your shoulders,' she told him. 'Don't let it get you down — we'll find a way.'

She kissed him then, and crept into his arms.

'After all,' she said, 'they're only animals! Bats, very similar to our own, only bigger. They're clever, and can use their minds in a way we can't, but they are still animals. Despite their telepathy, they have limitations. They eat and breathe and know emotion. They breed and care for their children and gossip amongst themselves. They have a weakness somewhere . . . and we'll find it!'

The dome, Vaughan thought; it's the dome that holds in their air and makes the colony possible. Smash that, and they've got to start all over again! The scientists of Earth were capable of producing a rocket capable of reaching the other side of the moon. It was one way to hit back; and he felt better for having thought of it.

Through the windows, the sun made a

brilliant splash of light in the dark void all about them. The moon had shrunk — and Earth loomed ahead. He could see cloud formations, like ice flows drifting on some unseen tide. The ship swooped down . . .

Vaughan and Ann stretched out on the floor, anticipating the landing. Over their heads, the stars shone — then the windows closed. Pressure built up as the ship resisted the pull of gravity. The darkness was like a blanket, smothering them, a blanket that grew heavier with every second.

The spaceship decelerated towards Earth.

Vaughan's mouth was forced open and he gulped for air. His brain was beginning to spin on that endless spiral which would bring unconsciousness. He was sweating under the strain, no longer aware of the ship's vibration; metal dug into him and he groaned, the sound echoing dully through his aching head.

Down and down . . . the pressure increasing all the time. Blackout was not far off. He tried to reach Ann's hand with his own but his arm was solid lead, immovable. The bat-people could stand greater deceleration and acceleration than Earthmen.

Earth — home — Paris. Evacuate Paris! The words ran unconnected through his brain. He must stay awake, get to a telephone and warn the Paris authorities. There might not be much time . . . three million people to save . . .

He could not do it. Rapidly increasing gravity beat him. The darkness closed in and swallowed him up as it might a drowning man. He was falling into a bottomless pit, every nerve shrieking in protest . . . evacuate Paris . . . then nothing . . .

14

Death of a City

He was lying on his back, staring up at a grey-blue sky dotted with puffs of white cloud. In the distance, an aeroplane droned by. It was peaceful, lying on the grassy bank under the trees with Ann by his side.

He shivered slightly; the sun went in and the breeze carried a damp coldness. He stretched himself, sitting up, pushing back lank black hair and smoothing his beard. He must have been asleep for he'd had a dream — nightmare would be a better word — a dream in which invaders from space . . .

He shook his head. His whole body ached; he was still sleepy, not fully conscious. He'd never felt so tired.

Ann lay like a log beside him, her honey-blonde hair awry, her skirt rucked up and one arm twisted under her.

Vaughan leant across and pulled down her skirt, kissed her lightly. She stirred in her sleep, but did not wake. He wondered, briefly, what they were doing there . . . his memory did not seem to be functioning properly.

Strange thoughts ran through his head. A flight to the moon — giant bats — missing uranium — a threat to destroy Paris. Each thought was isolated, disconnected, meaningless. He wanted to go back to sleep, but felt too cold.

Paris!

The word sounded like an alarm bell in his head, a trigger setting off the mechanism of memory. Consciousness returned with a rush, overwhelming him. He leapt to his feet. There was no sign of the spaceship — it must have left immediately after setting them down. He must get to a telephone . . .

He stooped and shook the girl vigorously.

'Ann — wake up!'

Her eyes opened, dazed, uncomprehending. She saw him, and her lips curved in a soft smile.

'Neil, darling — '

He shook her again, roughly.

'Ann. Remember Paris? I'm going to phone Irwin. Come after me.'

He turned, started running. He had no idea where he was and there didn't seem to be anybody to ask. He ran across a field, climbed a fence and found himself in a quiet lane. Trees bordered the far side and, beyond them, he saw smoke curling up from a farmhouse.

His heart thumped wildly as he pounded down the lane. If only he were in time . . .

He ran across the yard to the farmhouse. The front door stood open and he made straight for it. Seeing him, a buxom woman left the hens she was feeding, and called:

'What is it? Who do you want?'

Vaughan didn't stop. Seconds might count, and he'd already seen the telephone wires leading into the house. He was through the door, looking about him. The hall was tiled, littered with egg-boxes and pails, and there, against the wall, stood the telephone.

He lifted the receiver and rang the operator.

The buxom woman came through the door and stopped by his side.

'Has there been an accident?' she wanted to know.

'This is an emergency call,' Vaughan said. 'What part of the country am I in?'

'Why, Sussex, of course.' The woman looked at him as if he were crazy. 'This is Burke's farm, near Ditchling.'

The operator's voice came, bored: 'Number, please?'

Vaughan snapped out Irwin's number. 'And hurry, please. This is urgent.'

He fretted over the delay. Mechanical clicks came from the receiver. He heard his number repeated several times, then —

'Irwin speaking.'

'This is Neil Vaughan. I'm speaking from a farmhouse in Sussex, near Ditchling.'

'*Neil!* How — ?'

Vaughan cut in: 'Never mind that now. Listen! Is Paris still there?'

Irwin spluttered noisily.

'Is Paris — what? Of course Paris is still there! What the devil — '

Vaughan knew a moment's relief.

'Listen . . . I can't explain everything over the phone. You'll have to take my word. Paris must be evacuated immediately — the city and surrounding countryside. They are going to detonate a hydrogen bomb in the centre of the city!'

Irwin was silent.

Vaughan shouted: 'Can you hear me? You've got to do something right away.'

'Yes, I hear you, but it isn't so simple as that. The situation has degenerated while you've been away. I'll see what I can do . . . I'll see the Prime Minister immediately. Neil, you must come to Downing Street in person, and explain. Do you understand?'

'I'll be there in the hour,' Vaughan promised, 'but don't wait for me. Paris must be evacuated!'

He rang off, surprised to find Ann standing beside him.

'I've commandeered a car,' she said calmly. 'Come on!'

They ran outside and Vaughan slid

behind the wheel. Petrol tank three-quarters full. He stamped the accelerator into the floorboards. The buxom woman went back to her hens, shaking her head at such craziness.

Vaughan did not know exactly where he was so he headed north by the sun till he found a signpost pointing to London. He passed through Cuckfield and picked up the A23 at Handcross. With horn blaring, he held the car to the centre of the road on the Crawley by-pass. The needle of the speedometer flickered upwards. Sixty-five, seventy, seventy-five . . .

He jumped the traffic lights in Redhill and roared on to Purley. At the end of the Croydon by-pass, he had to slow down; he was approaching Streatham and Brixton, built-up areas busy with traffic. At Kennington, a police car gave chase, but Vaughan managed to stay ahead; explanations could wait.

He passed the Oval and shot over Westminster Bridge, turning right into Whitehall.

A police car swung into the curb

behind him as he and Ann jumped out of the car. There were two constables at the gate to Downing Street. Ann at his side, he showed his identification, and the police officer saluted.

'You are expected, sir. I have orders to admit you immediately.'

A few moments later they were inside 10 Downing Street. A servant showed them to a large room, where a number of men were grouped about a round table. The furniture was solid and old-fashioned, craftsmen-built.

Irwin was there, his hair greyer than before; the Prime Minister, an upright man with a stern face; the Minister of War and several others; almost a full cabinet, in fact. Stokes was a surprise — so was the Soviet ambassador.

The P.M. shook hands briskly.

'It is a considerable relief to know that you and Miss Delmar are safe,' he said. 'Your report, please. Essentials only — details can wait.'

Someone handed Vaughan a glass of brandy; he swallowed half, then talked quickly. Some faces showed incredulity as he spoke of their journey to the moon; he stressed the bat-people's mental powers, particularly their ability to teleport objects; he gave the ultimatum and warned then what would happen to Paris.

There was a stunned silence.

Ann said: 'Every word is true, gentlemen. We have our backs to the wall and are fighting for survival. Our only hope is unity — all nations must stand together.'

The Prime Minister rose to his feet.

'Mr. Vaughan, is there no hope of saving Paris? No steps we can take? Would an appeal to the interplanetary raiders be of any use?'

Vaughan shook his head.

'They are determined on a demonstration of power. Paris must be evacuated — and quickly. I have no idea how much time is left.'

The P.M. said, briefly: 'We shall fight, of course. Meanwhile, I will telephone Paris.'

He left the room; and Stokes and the Soviet ambassador followed him out, each anxious to report to his own government. The talk became general and Vaughan and Ann filled in some of the details.

The Prime Minister returned.

'I don't know . . . '

He stopped, turned to Vaughan.

'Of course, you can't know the present position. All over the world, governments are having difficulty in retaining power. The metal famine has created unemployment on a scale greater than anything known before. France is without a cabinet. I spoke to the Prefect, but he didn't seem prepared to accept responsibility.'

Vaughan said: 'I'll broadcast a warning — '

'No!' The Minister of War spoke sharply. 'In the present situation, I am against any public announcement. This is a matter for top-level discussion and — '

Ann Delmar rose, and snapped:

'You can't condemn more than three million people to death! We must broadcast a warning.'

The P.M. sighed.

'You're right of course,' he said. 'The people of the world must know what is going on. I will make an announcement myself; then you and Mr. Vaughan can speak. Translations will be broadcast simultaneously.'

The decision taken, Vaughan and Ann left with the Prime Minister for Broadcasting House. A studio was assigned to them, all radio and television broadcasting stopped. The announcer's voice went over the air:

We are interrupting all our television and radio programmes for a special announcement by the Prime Minister . . . '

The P.M. spoke briefly, from notes. He stated the position, then introduced Vaughan, who broadcast the alien ultimatum to the world. Ann spoke, confirming the truth of Vaughan's words, and the Prime Minister finished:

'Each one of you listening to me must try to understand what this means. We cannot accept the role of slave labourers to these interlopers from another world. We have no recourse except to enter into interplanetary war with the invaders. To the people of Paris, I have a few final words — leave your city! Do not delay for anything. Leave your possessions, your homes, your jobs. Take your families into the country. Now . . . hurry! At any moment, the hydrogen bomb may be exploded. Aid will be sent to you as soon as possible — and do not fear, we shall win through in the end!'

Outside Broadcasting House, Irwin waited with a car. He took charge of Vaughan and Ann, while the Prime Minister returned to Downing Street.

'Where are we going?' Ann asked as Irwin drove out of London.

'Into hiding. You are two very valuable people just now, and we are not taking chances with you. The information you alone have may be vital to winning the war; no one else has the least idea what we're up against.'

Vaughan frowned. It was logical, he supposed, but he didn't like the idea of running to ground.

Irwin drove fast up the North Road. Milestones flashed by, towns, villages. They left the main road and swung into a country lane.

'This hideaway was prepared a long

time back,' Irwin announced. 'It was to be Intelligence H.Q. in time of war — though we hadn't quite imagined a situation like this.'

He turned into the drive of a country house. There was a guard on the gate, but seeing Irwin, he waved them on. Inside the high walls, a lawn surrounded by flowerbeds reached to the house itself, a ramshackle affair badly in need of repair.

There was no external sign of the work that had been done. A lift shaft dropped from the dining hall deep into the ground. Below, under tons of rock and concrete, brightly lit corridors led to air-conditioned chambers. It was not a large establishment and there were few people actually in residence.

A meal waited for them and, afterwards, Irwin said:

'Rooms have been prepared for you. Get some sleep — this may be the last chance you'll have of sleeping, once things start to move.'

Vaughan lay on his bed. He didn't think he would sleep — there was so much on his mind. He just didn't know how tired he was.

★ ★ ★

The great exodus had started and all roads leading out of Paris were jammed to capacity. The bridges over the Seine were alive with scurrying humanity. Earth's greatest city resembled an anthill that had been kicked over, and the ants were leaving leaving . . .

It had not begun like that. At first, few people took heed of the warning. From Port Maillot, country buses left on schedule, carrying the first trickle of those who believed; expensive limousines roared out with those in authority, who were taking no chances. Special editions of newspapers were rushed on the streets, and the radio and TV warning broadcasts were endlessly repeated. Gradually more people began to pack up and leave.

In those first hours, it became a common sight to see motor vans and the occasional horse-and-cart, loaded with the family belongings and carrying a man and woman with their children. The youngsters enjoyed it; to them, the whole affair had the excitement of an adventure.

It was after the broadcasting stations fell silent that the panic commenced. Rumours started. Terror began to make itself felt. Suppose the warning were true? A hydrogen bomb set off in the centre of Paris . . .

The sun shone down on congested streets. The streams of cars and lorries swelled, almost choking the boulevards. Work gradually came to a standstill. On the Seine, launches and yachts weighed anchor and made away from the danger area. Aircraft took off with reckless regularity from airfields, resulting in several mid-air collisions. No ambulances attended the resultant crashes. The supply of taxis ran out, for no driver came back once he got clear of the city boundaries.

At the Louvre, a skeleton staff was trying to save precious art treasures. It was unthinkable that da Vinci's *Mona Lisa*, or the *Venus de Milo*, should be destroyed.

Schools were evacuated; hospitals

began to move those patients who could be moved. The police gave up the unequal struggle to control the traffic. A seething mass of humanity struggled outward from the city. They walked, they cycled, they clung to the outside of trains. Opera stars, cabaret dancers, apaches, people of all races rich and poor — they had but one idea. Leave Paris! There was fear mirrored in their faces, one thought in their heads . . . have we the time to escape?

The exodus degenerated to a mob fighting for existence. Vans were raided, goods chucked in the road as more and more people tried to climb aboard. The weak suffered, for now the madness had come. Every man for himself!

Metro and suburban trains did not return once they reached the outskirts. The Gare du Nord and the Gare St. Lazare were scenes of riots. From the quayside, men jumped into the river to swim to passing barges. In the Bois de Boulogne, racehorses were used to pull carts.

Fear drove them out. The noise of

sirens and hooters and bells joined the uproar of voices. More than three million people tried to get away . . .

By now, the heart of the city was deserted. It was quieter than a Sunday morning, the clamour of the mob a fading, distant thing. One last car raced under the Arc de Triomphe, on the way out from the doomed capital. In Notre Dame, a few people gathered for a final service, praying for a miracle to save the city . . . and in the gardens of the Tuileries a pair of lovers embraced and prepared to die in each other's arms.

A blind man tapped his way round an overturned car in the Place de la Concorde. On a hill in Montmartre, the sails of a windmill still turned. The last aircraft had left Le Bourget and a woman, demented by fear, threw herself from the top of the Eiffel Tower.

A dog howled, chasing in and out of the empty tables lining a boulevard in Montparnasse. The doors of the dress *salons* stood open and ribbons fluttered gaily, like flags at a last stand. The rich smell of restaurant kitchens attracted stray animals, while looters smashed plate glass windows in the Rue de Rivoli.

The sun continued to shine on Europe's loveliest of all cities. A strange quiet hung over the streets — it was almost as if the city itself knew . . . and waited.

Beyond Paris, the roads were choked with refugees. They made dark streamers that moved slowly, always outward from the centre. Fifty miles out, scientists had set up recording instruments to measure the force of the explosion; they were calm as they waited for the end.

A priest knelt to pray. An old woman, sick and forgotten, lay in her bed and sweated in fear. A drunken man reeled unsteadily from bar to bar, helping himself to bottles of wine.

The whole world waited . . .

It came suddenly, without warning.

A sheet of flame seared the sky. Paris erupted like a volcano and left a crater fifteen miles across. The explosion roared with a terrible thunder and the blast levelled everything in its path. The heat melted and the air boiled.

Then, slowly it seemed, a vast cloud of dust rose into the sky, climbing higher with every second, mushrooming out — a cloud of radioactive particles that destroyed life wherever they settled.

A mile high rose the plume of death . . . ten miles, eleven, twelve . . . carried on the tempestuous winds that were an aftermath of the bomb. Invisible radiation killed and maimed those in its path. The physicists' recording instruments were shattered.

Across the Channel, people winced as the shock wave hit them. By radio, word was carried round the globe:

'Paris is gone!'

There was a long sadness — and fear. The moon raiders had kept their word. What now? What would happen now? Must humanity submit to the invaders?

They were questions that no one dared to answer.

15

The Razor's Edge

Someone shook him, gently but firmly. Vaughan opened his eyes and saw Irwin standing over him.

'Get dressed, Neil — breakfast is waiting. We're flying to attend a meeting of the United Nations.'

Vaughan said: 'Paris?'

Irwin nodded soberly, spreading his hands.

'Gone! And God alone knows how many people with it. The death toll must run into hundreds of thousands.'

Vaughan could not think about it. He washed and dressed and made his way to the dining room. Ann was already there, sipping black coffee — a plate of ham and eggs in front of her, untouched. He guessed how she felt; he, too, had lost all desire for food since hearing of the destruction of Paris.

Irwin came in. 'Ready?'

They rose together and left the room. A lift-cage carried them to the surface, and sunshine. There was a car standing in the drive and Irwin took the wheel: Vaughan and Ann sat silently m the back. No one had anything to say on the journey to the airfield.

They stopped once, at a store in a small village. A crowd had gathered, listening to the voice of an announcer on the radio that was being relayed throughout the store.

' . . . medical aid has been rushed to France from a score of countries. The English Channel is full of ships from naval vessels to river steamers, ferrying the injured across to emergency hospitals set up along the south coast. Doctors and nurses have flown in to help. Belgium has organized rest centres for the homeless, and wagon-loads of orphaned children have been taken to Germany. The American Red Cross is flying two hundred hospital-aircraft across the Atlantic. The Swiss Government have appealed for food, clothing and bedding to help refugees.

'Observers, flying as close to the scene of the disaster as conditions permit, report that literally nothing is left of the city. Paris has vanished as if it never existed. The countryside, for a distance of fifty miles all round is blighted. The sky is still not clear of dust; a grey pall hangs over everything and wind is still dispersing radioactive matter over a wide area. Scientists state that it will be many weeks before the full extent of damage can be reckoned . . . '

The listeners did not move or speak. They stood in silence, overwhelmed by the catastrophe. The woman behind the counter showed no sign that she knew Vaughan was there. He paid for his purchase at the till and walked out.

They reached the airport in fifteen minutes. A plane was ready and they left immediately.

Vaughan said: 'Fly over the Channel. Get as close as you can.'

The pilot headed his plane to the south. Beyond London, the roads showed continuous streams of traffic, taking refugees inland and supplies to the coast. From Dover to Portsmouth, harbours and ports were alive with shipping; smaller craft landed on the beaches. Over the sea, fishing boats, private yachts and pleasure craft joined naval ships in ferrying the injured and the homeless to safety. Vaughan had never seen so many ships.

The French coast, from Dunkirk to Cherbourg, was a heartbreaking scene. Crowds swarmed the beaches waiting to be taken off. Le Havre was jammed with shipping, the harbour almost blocked. Hospitals and rest centres, field kitchens. Inland, it was grimmer still; mass burials were taking place, and there was no time for identification or mourning. Several thousand bodies had to be disposed of before plague broke out . . .

The plane swung to the west, avoiding the dust cloud that hung over the area of devastation, then climbed into the stratosphere and headed out for the Atlantic.

Vaughan said, slowly: 'Do you realize

that if we had not made the hydrogen bomb, this could never have happened? I'm convinced the moon raiders have no such weapons.'

Neither Ann nor Irwin answered him. The plane droned on, the hours passed. The radio brought them fresh news:

'Whatever world governments may decide, city dwellers are taking matters into their own hands. Thousands of people are leaving their homes and moving into open country. Capitals all over the world are emptying. New York is virtually deserted. No one wants to be where the next bomb falls . . . '

And later:

'The invaders no longer hide behind a veil of secrecy; their spaceships have been seen in full daylight. Over Berlin and Rome, London and Moscow and Peking, Ottawa and Washington and Rio, flying saucers watch the skies. Guided missiles and fighter planes sent against them explode before they can come within effective range: scientists say the alien vessels are protected by an energy-screen that so far is impenetrable.'

The plane was a moving shadow across the blue-green ocean. The radio continued:

'A supply of cobalt has been taken from Ontario. This time, there was no mystery about its vanishing. A ship landed in full view and huge bats were seen. No action was taken against them for fear of reprisals.

'Special news flash! Uranium 235 was removed from an atomic plant in Russia, states our Moscow correspondent. No details are available.'

The pilot put the plane into a long glide on approaching Long Island. Lower, over Manhattan, Vaughan saw empty sidewalks. It looked as peaceful as a summer's day in the heart of the country.

Stokes was waiting for them. He said to Ann:

'Your family have moved to Louisville and are staying with your Aunt Maude. They hope you'll join them when you can.'

Ann nodded.

'I'm glad they've gone, Richard. They'll be safer there.'

The United Nations building over-looked an empty river; a few uniformed soldiers were on guard, but there was little traffic. The silence was somehow frightening.

'It's like a morgue,' Stokes grumbled. 'I never thought I'd see the day when New York would look like this. I doubt if there's anyone left except the delegates to this meeting — and some of those haven't shown up.'

Vaughan smiled faintly. An elliptical shadow appeared on the concrete road-way, and he looked up. A raider spaceship hovered there, waiting . . .

'I don't think there's much danger,' he said. 'The bat-folk want metal — and they're more likely to get that if an effective government is in control here. They're not fools, so they'll leave us alone.'

In the council chamber, the meeting took place in a sombre atmosphere. No one laughed when Vaughan told of his journey to the moon and how the ultimatum had been presented to him; the destruction of Paris had shown

226

everyone that the situation was critical. They listened in complete silence, apprehensive; more than one member gazed up through the big windows to the ship in the sky.

Like the sword of Damocles, Vaughan thought.

Russians and Americans were united now, and no one mentioned an unstable gold standard; there were other, more important things to consider. This time, there were no wisecracks about 'comic-strips' and Martians.

Vaughan answered questions put to him. New means of helping France were proposed. The meeting dragged on . . . and it seemed that the real purpose of the assembly was shunned. No one wanted to admit that Earth was helpless.

The Soviet delegate rose and said bluntly:

'Mr. Chairman, I understand that this meeting was called to decide a course of action. We have been given an ultimatum — supply the moon raiders with the metals they require, or be exterminated. So far, no plan to grapple with this emergency has been put forward.'

He paused. In the silence, the member for India shuffled his feet. Outside, visible through the windows of that high, vaulted chamber, a giant bat flitted across the sky, perpetual reminder of the menace that had come to Earth.

'What happened to Paris can obviously happen to the rest of the world,' continued the Russian. 'We have no means of fighting back. I propose, therefore, that the situation be accepted, that we agree to supply metals as required. The structure of our own society must be adapted accordingly. If anyone present has an alternative to offer, let him speak now.'

'My people will never surrender!' cried the swarthy member of a small South American state, springing to his feet. 'We must fight for freedom — slavery cannot be tolerated!'

No one took him seriously.

The chairman said: 'We will vote on the motion of the member for the Union of Soviet Socialist Republics.'

Hands were raised, but there was no

need of counting — with but one dissentient, the motion was carried and Earth capitulated. The assembly broke up.

Vaughan and Ann, with Irwin and Stokes, drove to an army camp where they had a meal. They slept through the afternoon and were wakened as dusk fell.

New York was a city of darkness and silence, a dead place. Vaughan wondered: how many other cities are like this tonight? It gave him an eerie feeling to think of those deserted capitals, the encampments that must have formed on grassy plains and hillsides, far from civilization. How were those people living? Had they any food? What was to happen to them?

Stokes said: 'We're ready to leave now.'

Vaughan didn't know what was coming. Secret orders had arrived during the day, but no one spoke of them. They drove to an airport. A plane was waiting and it took off immediately, flying without lights into the northern sky. It crossed the Great Lakes and passed over Canada, heading westward.

Darkness closed in, hiding the ground below. Their route lay over Saskatchewan and Alberta, and dawn was still some way off when they reached the Rocky Mountains. The pilot took the plane down, under a belt of rain-clouds. No lights showed; radar guided the plane in to land, and it bumped over a grassy plain, a valley between high mountains.

Rain streamed across the landscape, blanketing everything in grey gloom. A lone figure in a wet slicker loomed out of the dark.

'Follow me — it's not far.'

They trudged through the rain, the ground turning to mud under their feet. Presently, a wooden shack showed up; beyond that, the workings of a derelict mine. It was a secret place.

A tunnel led into the base of the mountains and they passed along it, out of the rain. Deeper and deeper the shaft led, opening out in a natural hollow under the rock. Here a few men were gathered about a rough table; oil lamps burned, and hardwood benches served as seating accommodation.

Vaughan grunted, impressed. He saw the stern, upright figure of Britain's Prime Minister, the lanky, silver-haired President of the United States; and, representing Russia, a huge man in a fur coat who looked like a great shaggy bear. He knew then, it was this secret meeting deep in the Rocky Mountains that would decide the fate of Earth — the United Nations assembly counted for nothing.

The blonde uncommunicative Fedora was also present; she gave no sign that she had seen Vaughan before.

The meeting began without preliminaries.

'Mr. Vaughan,' said the Prime Minister, 'and you too, Miss Delmar, have been brought here to provide certain information. As you now realize, the meeting in New York was no more than a mask for our activities. Certainly, we must provide some supplies for the invaders — that is inevitable — but we do not intend to give up without a struggle. We are met to decide what action to take. New weapons must be created, a plan made. We rely on you to give a lead . . . '

Questions followed, and Vaughan and Ann answered as best they could. There were pauses while something was translated for the man in the fur coat. The hours passed steadily, Vaughan and Ann going slowly and thoroughly over everything they had seen on the moon.

'Very well,' decided the Prime Minister at length, 'the problem resolves itself into two phases: one, the base on the moon, without which the aliens will certainly be severely handicapped; two, their incredible mental powers. Teleportation gives them an advantage which — at present — I see no way of overcoming. The moon base, on the other hand, is a material target, even though remote. I suggest that we concentrate all our efforts on destroying it.'

'It occurred to me,' Vaughan put in, 'that we might construct a spaceship capable of carrying a hydrogen bomb, and of reaching the moon. If we can guide it to the moon base on the far side of the moon, one hydrogen bomb would destroy it utterly.'

'But how would the rocket get through

to actually strike the alien base?' one of the President's aides objected. 'Surely the aliens will have their protective energy screens in operation around it? Just as they have around their spaceships here on Earth? We've already tried and failed to fire missiles at their craft.'

'Our scientists have established that these so-called energy screens work by directly releasing the energy of the *air*,' Vaughan answered, emphasizing his last word. 'The freely-moving molecules that make up our atmosphere have tremendous kinetic energy. The aliens are able to transform that energy into heat. But the moon has no such atmosphere: we believe that their base there will not be protected in that way.'

The P.M. smiled faintly.

'I had the same idea in mind.' He turned briskly to his colleagues. 'Well, gentlemen, is it practicable? Can we build and send such a ship to the moon?'

There was silence and, to Vaughan, it was obvious that both the American President and the Soviet leaders were reluctant to speak in front of each other.

The situation forced them together, but there was, even now, a lack of mutual trust.

Britain's Prime Minister spoke again.

'Come, gentlemen, the fate of Earth rests in our hands. Co-operation is essential. I am prepared to state for my country and our European partners that we will make available our scientists and technicians who are presently involved in the peaceful exploration of space with interplanetary probes and satellites. And we already know that both the United States and Russia have sent rockets to the moon, including manned missions of peaceful exploration. So the only question is: can we quickly mount a *military* mission?'

Fedora translated for the man in the fur coat:

'Russia too is willing to pool our information and technical resources.'

'The United States,' added the President, 'has already sent manned and unmanned expeditions to the moon, and around it. Between us, it should certainly prove feasible to carry out such a military objective on the far side of the moon.'

The Prime Minister rubbed his hands.

'Good! It remains then, only to settle details. The work on the project must be kept secret at all costs. I suggest that several groups operate independently of each other, technical liaison being effected by one scientist from each country. Underground bases, remote from cities, are essential. And speed . . . we must strike at the earliest possible moment.'

It was decided that Ann Delmar should remain in America while Vaughan flew back to England. Between them, they represented the sum of Earth's information about the invaders, and, as such, were two very important people — too important to be allowed to remain together in the present emergency. If anything should happen to one, the other must be doubly safeguarded . . .

'We are balanced,' stated the Prime Minister, 'on a razor s edge. We must fight to save ourselves — yet open revolt can bring only disaster. One slip may well be fatal.'

It was a sobering thought.

Vaughan took Ann aside, and kissed her.

'We'll meet again,' he said, 'when it's over. This situation can't last forever, and we've a chance now — '

Her response startled him.

'Must it always be like this, Neil, two opposing forces making war?' There was a note of bitterness in her voice. 'They have so much to give us — why couldn't we work together? We have metals they need; they must have incredible scientific knowledge to pass on. Why do we have to fight?'

Why, indeed, Vaughan thought; if only we could have a means of making ourselves understood . . .

16

Under Alien Domination

Vaughan gave a long sigh. He was tired, his head ached, and he badly wanted to see Ann again. For a month, he had been confined to that underground hideaway in the Midlands, and he was sick of artificial lighting and concrete corridors and the background purr of ventilation motors. He felt an urge to see the sun, to feel the wind on his face and tramp long miles over the hills.

It had not been an idle month. Each day, he was closeted with scientific experts who questioned him on every facet of the bats' civilization. He talked to chemists and biologists, engineers and historians, psychologists and rocket technicians, physicists and zoologists; a dossier was compiled, listing every detail Vaughan could recall of his contact with the aliens.

The Intelligence centre rapidly became headquarters for the group planning resistance to the invaders. Reports came in a steady stream; reports of metals handed over, of a new landing by the bats, of secret rocket construction in America and Russia. The Prime Minister was a frequent visitor, even though the seat of government had been moved out of London. The news from France was bad. Radioactivity continued to spread outwards from the explosion area, and a strange sickness swept the land. It affected animals as well as humans, and no quarantine could contain it. Doctors worked feverishly to find an antidote to what newspapers called the 'Paris Plague'.

City life had come to a halt and vast, straggling encampments spread across the countryside. Inevitably there was trouble; little shelter in bad weather, lack of food and water. Riots were frequent and the government was forced to use soldiers to maintain order. In the U.S. a starving mob attacked a military camp and more than a hundred people lost their lives in the fighting.

Civilization tottered on the brink of chaos. Power supplies failed and means of communication broke down. It became difficult even to keep factories running to provide the invaders with enough metal to buy time in the fight for freedom.

Max Woodroffe became active again. Vaughan had lost sight of him in the greater struggle, but Woodroffe had not been idle. He was still after personal power, and although his organization had been largely dispersed, he appeared from time to time in an attempt to overthrow governments throughout the world.

His attempt at organizing the refugees from the cities failed. A hungry mob is no respecter of persons and Woodroffe had not the supplies to satisfy them. He moved on, then, to the factories producing metals for the invaders, and engineered strikes until the army chased him out.

And, all the while, in a hundred secret bases, work went on to complete the ship that would carry a hydrogen bomb to the moon . . .

Fresh orders came from the bat-people. Uranium 235 was needed, so the atomic plants must be kept working. Copper too, was required in large quantities. When they had orders to give, someone was teleported to a lonely place, where a solitary bat appeared to put pictures into the mind of the helpless victim — after which he was returned to pass on their instructions.

In the Soviet Union, a spaceship landed close by one of the metal-producing factories — and was immediately attacked by angry workers. The ship took off, and, minutes later, a hydrogen bomb was teleported to the area.

The factory and the workers simply disappeared . . . and no one ever attacked a giant bat again.

Vaughan had plenty of time to think, and his thoughts always returned to Ann's bitter tirade against war. It was a mood that continually came to him, and he could not shake it off. Why did two civilizations have to fight immediately they made contact? True, communication with the bat-people was difficult, but he did not feel that was the answer. Something might have been worked out — except for the fact that the moon raiders considered the human race fit only to supply their needs.

He suggested to the government that he be allowed to try to find a way of cooperating with the bats — but the idea was instantly vetoed. So Earth continued under the yoke of the bat-people's domination.

★ ★ ★

The increasing difficulties of living in the open eventually drove people back to the cities. Life slowly resumed its old pattern but, now, under the shadow of fear. In the sky, enemy ships hovered and giant bats were seen flying. Schools re-opened and hospitals got on with the job of fighting for individual lives; working for their daily bread again became important to men. The drift back to the cities went on . . .

An independent observer might have been surprised at the speed with which the human race adapted itself to the new conditions; radio stations once more turned out popular music and comedy shows; sport had a sudden boom. People no longer spoke of the menace hanging over them — though a certain grimness was apparent in the faces of workmen and their families when another batch of metal was delivered to the raiders. No one used the word 'slavery,' but it was in everyone's thoughts.

Demand and supply — the price of existence, with Earth reduced to the role of a satellite world.

Vaughan and Irwin were often together, and they discussed at length the situation that might exist after the destruction of the moon colony. Irwin was optimistic, believing the invaders would leave us alone. Vaughan didn't feel so sure. It seemed to him that the moon had only been chosen as a base because the bats had preferred to operate secretly; there was no need of that now. He wondered if they would descend on Earth and take over entirely. It was not a pleasant thought.

Reports continued to come in from all

parts of the world, and one day Irwin handed Vaughan a message that read:

'Mexico, Tuesday. Workmen at a silver mine in the Lobos Hills today turned on a group of agitators who were trying to induce them to strike. It appears that a Union official warned off the agitators, who struck him to the ground. Instantly, a riot started; the mood of the workmen, who had been listening docilely to propaganda speeches, changed to one of violence. Before the police could interfere, the agitators had been lynched. One of the dead men has been identified as Maximillian Woodroffe.'

Vaughan smiled grimly as he handed back the report.

'I can't say I'm sorry. He got what he was asking for — and from people he tried to use for his own ends. Well, that's one trouble-maker less in the world.'

Irwin nodded.

'That's the way I feel — I only wish we could get rid of these damned bats as easily!'

The days passed. In a letter to Vaughan, Ann said that she would be flying over soon — and that she would like to be married.

'My darling,' she wrote, 'I am not at all confident that our plan will succeed, and, if the worst happens, I want to be at your side, and to enjoy some short measure of happiness . . . '

While Vaughan wanted to marry her, the letter depressed him. One phrase rang in his head like an alarm bell:

'If the worst happens . . . '

Suppose the bat-folk *knew* — and it was not unlikely with their telepathic powers — of Earth's plan to smash the moon base, and were simply waiting for the right moment to strike? The idea tortured him. What kind of life would be left for the survivors of the reprisals that would surely follow? The planet could not support an indefinite number of hydrogen bomb explosions; already two vast tracts of country were uninhabitable. Dare we destroy all the H-bombs in the world?

He showed Ann's letter to Irwin, who took a different view.

'She's in love with you,' the M.I.5 chief

said; 'naturally she wants to marry — that's all there is to it. If the invaders suspected how close our moon-ship is to completion, they'd have done something before this. Stop worrying, Neil. You're going to be very happy with Ann.'

The day before Ann was due to arrive, the Prime Minister visited the hideout. He was in good spirits.

'Any time now, we shall be ready to fire the rocket. Work has proceeded at a terrific pace and the final assembly is complete. At this moment the ship is being fuelled and the instruments tested. It will be a robot ship, of course, flying a pre-determined orbit — nothing can save the moon base once the ship leaves Earth.'

Vaughan began to hope again.

The P.M. stayed with them, waiting for news to come in.

In the underground hideout, tension increased as zero hour approached. Coded reports came in a constant flow. Operation Freedom, as the project was officially labelled, was about to be launched. Scientists had finished last minute checks and all was ready. The minutes ticked by . . .

Vaughan waited tensely. Irwin tired of pacing the room and sat down before the radio that kept them in touch with the firing base, an isolated part of the jungle in Equatorial Africa. Somewhere a white-coated scientist crouched over the button that would fire the ship, waiting for the right moment.

Vaughan tried to imagine the scene; the natural camouflage of giant trees and broad-ribbed leaves; the moist, sticky heat; the brightness of the sky; perhaps, some way off, the beating of native tom-toms — and the ship, poised in a clearing, its nose pointed for the moon. He imagined the scientists in a concrete firing post; and the technicians who would, by this time, have left the area.

The P.M. consulted his watch. Five minutes to go . . . he switched over direct to the control room in distant Africa.

The radio came to life.

'Stand by for firing.'

A long pause, an eternity for those waiting.

246

'Four minutes . . . '

Irwin jumped up and began his pacing again.

'Three minutes . . . two minutes . . . one . . . '

Vaughan held his breath. The Prime Minister's lips moved in silent prayer.

'Fifty seconds to go . . . forty . . . thirty . . . '

Vaughan imagined a hand poised over the firing button.

'Twenty. Ten. Nine. Eight. Sev — '

The radio went dead.

Irwin swore. The Premier grabbed for an outside phone.

'Get me Greenwich observatory! Hurry!'

The connection was made. The P.M. said, urgently:

'Do you see it?'

A minute passed. Two minutes. Then the Prime Minister replaced the telephone.

'Nothing,' he said wearily. 'Something's gone wrong. If the ship had left on time, it would be visible in the sky. There's nothing.'

A radio mechanic fiddled with their set.

'No trouble here,' he stated. 'Transmitting station must be out of action.'

Vaughan sat down. There was nothing to do except wait. Questions teemed through his brain. What had happened at that lonely outpost? If only he knew for certain . . .

The P.M. was at the phone again, making a long-distance call.

'I'm in touch with an R.A.F. station in South Africa,' he said. 'They're sending a jet plane over the area. We should get a report within minutes.'

An amplifier was hurriedly rigged to broadcast the message. Ten minutes passed, then the sound of the pilot's voice was heard, fading and rising through the crackle of atmospherics.

'I've never seen anything like this — the whole jungle is on fire! A hundred miles of forest burning — smoke blotting out most of the view. Now I see it! A crater — and what a crater! Must be all of fifteen miles across. This is hell . . . dust and smoke . . . a blazing fury sweeping across the jungle.'

The Prime Minister switched off. His

face was grey, haggard. No one spoke. The silence was like a living thing.

Vaughan thought dully: They knew — they *knew* all the time, and just waited; then, at the critical moment teleported another bomb.

Irwin said: 'This is the end, then. There's no use, even in building another ship. We can't get at their base . . . ever!'

The Premier made a wry face.

'Well, gentlemen,' he said, 'we tried — and failed. I don't see what more we can do. Earth is no longer ours . . . it has passed into the hands of the invader!'

17

The Weapon

Twenty-four hours went by, and the bat-people made no reprisals. The underground H.Q. had been abandoned, personnel dispersed; Vaughan and Irwin were staying at a small hotel in Cornwall.

Newspapers carried the story of the African bomb, but no news had been released on the failure of the moon-ship project. The world wondered, and the few in the know waited. Forty-eight hours — and still nothing happened.

'They're ignoring us,' Irwin said glumly. 'We're just not important enough for them to bother with — a minor irritation, if that. They've destroyed the threat to their base and are content to let us go on supplying metals. The whole human race isn't big enough to be dangerous to them . . . '

Vaughan nodded, remembering how he

and Ann had been ignored on the moon. The bats were sure of their superiority and acted accordingly.

They were sitting on the veranda of their hotel, looking down on a small harbour. It was peaceful, just the blue of the water, the smooth lines of boats, the white, flitting forms of gulls. Not a hint of an alien menace anywhere.

Vaughan's thoughts turned to Ann. She was overdue, and he was anxious about her. The last letter he'd received hinted that she had good reason for the delay, which she would explain on her arrival. Vaughan couldn't help being jealous; Stokes was in love with Ann, and he was in America. Perhaps . . . he tried to put the thought out of his head. Ann would be true to him, but . . . America was a long way off.

Irwin, sipping a lager beer, watched him across the table, and smiled.

'Forget it, Neil,' he said gently. 'Ann will be here soon, and you'll be married.'

Vaughan started, his face reddening. He didn't like to think that his feelings were so obvious. He rose and leaned over the veranda rail, looking down into the harbour; the tide was out, boats lay at odd angles; a gull pecked at a piece of decayed fish in the mud.

'I guess you're right. Only it's this not knowing. Ann should have been here yesterday, and I can't imagine what is keeping her away. After all, it's her idea . . . '

'Must be something important,' Irwin said thoughtfully. But he lapsed into silence and did not continue.

Vaughan filled his pipe and resolved not to let his thoughts dwell on Richard Stokes.

Another day passed; then he received a message that Ann would be arriving by plane at London Airport later that day.

Vaughan packed hurriedly, called Irwin, and started the car. He drove through Exeter and on to Salisbury striking north to pick up the Bath road, arriving at the airport before Ann's plane landed from America. He waited with Irwin in the reception hall.

The place was curiously deserted; the threat of enemy occupation had adversely affected air travel. Only one plane came in while they waited, and the ground staff were restless. They gave the impression that it was not aircraft for which they waited.

Irwin and Vaughan ate sandwiches and drank black coffee while they waited. The TV monitors in the lounge showed that a British Airways Boeing 747 was due to land within the next ten minutes.

They gulped down the last of their coffee and, together, they moved to the reception barrier. The sound of engines came from the sky.

Irwin, squinting up through the sunlight, grunted: 'There she is — coming in now.'

Vaughan saw the glint of a silvered fuselage; then incredibly swiftly it seemed, the 747 touched down, wheels bouncing on the concrete runway. The plane taxied towards the control tower and the engines cut off. Two passengers alighted.

Vaughan's pulse leapt; he had to restrain an impulse to leap the barrier and run to take Ann in his arms. He recognized her easily, despite the distance. Her blonde hair was tied back with a ribbon, and she wore a bright red jumper with a two-piece suit. He waved, and she waved back.

Then she turned to the man at her side. Vaughan could not make him out clearly, but he was certain it was not Stokes. This man was slimmer, with close-cropped hair and spectacles. It seemed they had a lot of luggage, for a collection of wooden crates was transferred from the plane to a waiting car. Vaughan fretted impatiently.

Minutes passed. Irwin went back to his seat. The car was gradually loaded, and drove slowly to the reception building. There was the usual passport and customs procedure — not even an invasion from another planet could change that — then Ann was walking towards him.

Vaughan gathered her in his arms and kissed her, and the man with the packing cases looked the other way. Finally, laughing, Ann pushed Vaughan off and smoothed out her clothes.

'Professor Dobson,' she said briskly. 'Neil Vaughan and Mr. Irwin — both of the British Intelligence Service.'

Dobson was clean-shaven, freckled, not more than thirty. He had a friendly grin.

He said, 'Pleasure to meet you,' and shook hands.

Ann looked critically at Vaughan. 'You're looking well,' she murmured, 'but, darling, your beard badly needs trimming!'

She lowered her voice: 'I think we've got it, Neil — the weapon to beat the bats . . .'

Vaughan felt carefully round the inside of his mouth with his tongue, suddenly afraid to ask anything.

Irwin said: 'In those cases?'

Dobson drawled: 'That's just extra equipment, for experimental purposes.' His accent was Texan. He patted the small metal case he carried in one hand. 'The real box of tricks is here.'

Ann explained: 'That's why I was delayed. I told you I didn't think the moon-rocket would work out, so I began to think along new lines. Dobson has been helping me. We've already given one demonstration to the United States government and they've agreed to go ahead with research on it. There'll be a lot to do before we can go into action. The next move is to see someone in authority here, and explain what we're doing.'

Irwin nodded.

'I can arrange that, Miss Delmar. I'll get on the phone right away.'

He hurried off, and Vaughan looked hard at Ann.

'Is this going to mean another hydrogen bomb attack?' he asked bluntly.

She didn't answer at once. Finally, she gave a shrug of her shoulders.

'Perhaps. Isn't that something we have to risk? Do you want our children to grow up as slaves to these creatures from the moon?'

Dobson said, eagerly: 'We've worked it out. Research cells all over the world, working along independent lines, but each in contact with the others. We wouldn't try to keep it dead secret — that's been tried, and failed. The idea is to have so many units that all of them can't possibly be wiped out. One must succeed.'

Vaughan said: 'But they knew about the moon-rocket. How?' A thought nagged at the back of his mind. It was connected with his car crash.

'Wait.'

He thought back to their interview with the elder bat on the moon. A lot of things had been explained then; but there was something —

'Of course! They can take on human form ... which means they've been masquerading as Earthmen, and learning our plans direct at the source. There must be spies in the government!'

He looked suspiciously at Dobson; even Ann could be one of them.

'They can't really change form,' Ann said calmly. 'It can only be an illusion they create telepathically. A visual image impressed on our minds by the power of thought — and we can easily detect that. Like this!'

She reached out a hand and touched Vaughan, felt the cloth of his coat, and his hand; repeated the process with Dobson.

'They'll still feel alien to this Earth,' she explained, 'no matter how they appear. Besides, they cannot shed their peculiar odour.'

'And I guess that takes care of that problem,' the professor grunted.

Irwin came back, and was startled when Vaughan grabbed hold of him. Ann explained quickly; and Irwin returned immediately to the telephone to pass on this new information.

A plane was chartered, and after Dobson's crates had been stored, the party flew to Scotland. It was evening when they landed at a small airfield in the Highlands and a car took them to Glenferry, where the government had taken refuge in a castle overlooking Loch Strathaire.

It was a wild, desolate place, with mountains in the background and miles of heather-covered moors; a land of rock and sparse cultivation, of forest and river and salmon run. The castle, gloomy in grey twilight, was built right on the edge of the loch, a towering crag of stone, mossy and weather-beaten.

There were lights showing from the ground floor windows and cars parked in the drive. A security man carefully felt their person with his hands before allowing them through to the main chamber. There, the Prime Minister and a few select members of the cabinet had gathered to hear what the American contingent had to say.

Ann introduced Dobson and began to speak.

'The moon raiders have proved that their power of mind is greater than any material weapon which we can turn against them. Teleportation is the one thing that gives them an advantage — so I looked for a method of nullifying that advantage. It was obvious that no human being has telepathic powers of the order we need to fight back, but it occurred to me that some mechanism might be evolved which would 'amplify' human thought.'

She paused, looking round her; but she need not have feared ridicule. The British government had reached a stage when it was prepared to consider any method of combating the invader, no matter how fantastic it might appear at first. She had the attention of every person in the room as she continued:

'We have come to think of the bats as something supernatural — yet they are only animals who can use their minds in a way we do not understand. Destroy their power to teleport solid matter, and we destroy their power over us! It is basically as simple as that . . . though putting the idea into practice will not be at all simple. However, that is the line I have been following.

'We know little about telepathic communication, but it is very probably energy released in the form of a wave-motion, akin to electromagnetic waves. The first thing that struck me was that some work had already been done in a not entirely dissimilar field — I refer to electro-encephalography — and I decided to go to an expert. That is how I came to meet Professor Dobson; and I found he had the same idea. In fact, he had already started experiments and, in due course, I introduced him to the President, who sanctioned funds for considerable research. The professor will now talk about his work.'

Ann sat down and Dobson rose. He spoke with an easy drawl, punctuating his remarks by gestures of his hands.

'First, gentlemen, let me emphasize the difference between my normal work in encephalography and the project on which we are about to embark. The human brain gives off minute electrical impulses that it is possible to record and measure on delicate instruments; this is used in hospitals as an aid to detecting certain disorders of the brain. The exact relationship of these impulses to thought is not entirely known.

'I am working on an 'amplifier' to increase the strength of these impulses and I have found that — theoretically — there is no limit to the possible amplification. A lot of work remains to be done but, essentially, we propose to construct a machine that will broadcast human thought-waves. This field of energy, it is hoped, will interfere with the telepathic communication of the invaders

261

and render them powerless.

'As you will see, what we are attempting to do is blanket the thought-waves of the giant bats, to construct a screen of energy, a barrier which will stop them teleporting hydrogen bombs or anything else. If we are successful, their advantage is gone and we can fight back with all the weapons we possess. And I do not doubt that we shall win!'

Dobson stopped, leaned on the table with both hands, and said quietly:

'I cannot, of course, guarantee that such an energy field will stop the aliens teleporting — but I do consider it a project worth trying. In America, we have already started work on the necessary research; it will increase our chances if you, too, instigate a similar programme. And now, I am going to give a simple demonstration which, I hope, will show that your time and energy will not be wasted in following up my remarks.'

He opened his case and brought out something that looked like a small television set, fitted with a screen and control unit.

'I shall need a volunteer . . . '

Vaughan left his chair and stepped forward.

'Right — sit here.' Dobson dragged a chair up to his equipment. 'You've nothing to fear, it's quite harmless.'

He brought a metal helmet from his case and fitted it over Vaughan's head.

'Electrodes touch the scalp, picking up thought impulses, which are fed through the amplifier. This is a battery-operated unit; from a mains supply, I could get better results. Watch, please!'

He switched on and a wavy line flickered on the screen.

'The impulses are fed directly through the wires to the screen. Now I am going to broadcast them.'

He took another instrument from his case and placed it on a table at the end of the room.

'I am going to step up the power. You see the readings on the display here?' He pointed. 'They indicate the different levels of energy. Look there — that increase shows the amplifier is working! Now, watch the instrument across the room.'

For a few seconds, the second screen remained blank, then, as Dobson increased power, a wavy line showed, a replica of that on the first screen.

'What has happened,' Dobson explained, 'is that I have succeeded in broadcasting thought-impulses from Mr. Vaughan's brain. There is no direct connection between transmitter and receiver — only a wave-motion through the air, similar to that of radio.'

He switched off and removed the helmet from Vaughan's head.

'That finishes the demonstration, gentlemen. Not very impressive, perhaps, but I hope I have indicated the possibilities. It is for you to decide whether you develop the idea.'

There was a moment's silence. Then someone asked:

'When the second screen operated, do I understand that the space between transmitter and receiver was filled by — er — thought radiations?'

'That is correct,' Dobson agreed.

'And the thought-waves filled this room? Permeating the air about ourselves? Yet I felt nothing! Surely, if it does not affect us, it will not interfere with the invaders — how do you explain that, professor?'

Dobson said, simply: 'We are not telepathic. What I am hoping is that a powerful, fully-developed screen of radiation will prevent the bats from using their powers over a distance. We can only try it out; there is no other way of testing my theory.'

Again there was silence. The members of the cabinet looked at each other, then to the Prime Minister for guidance. He smiled faintly.

'It seems worth trying,' he said carefully. 'We have little to lose — perhaps much to gain. I recommend that every facility be given Professor Dobson to develop this weapon.'

After that, the meeting discussed details and assigned helpers to the professor. It was not till the early hours of the morning that anyone went to bed; there was a new spirit abroad and hopes were high. Earth had been given a weapon with which to fight back . . . we might yet throw off the yoke of oppression.

The next day was a busy one. Dobson wanted equipment and technical assistants; a working schedule had to be planned; different areas assigned to various groups; the whole project organized so that each party knew the development programme of the others. Vaughan, Ann Delmar, and Irwin acted as liaison officers, while Dobson flew to the Soviet to put the new plan before the Russians and enlist their aid.

'This business is too technical for me to follow,' Irwin said, after a long session with the scientists. 'It's out of our hands now. I'm going to give you two weeks leave, Neil — you've worked hard on this job, and it's time you rested; besides, you and Ann have your own plans, and there's no need to put off your marriage. By the time you get back, we may be ready to strike the first blow — and there's nothing any of us can do until the experts hand us the results of their work.'

Vaughan looked at Ann; and she slipped her hand into his and smiled.

'I'm ready, Neil. Mr. Irwin is right — we can't do any more.'

266

It was a quiet wedding and, after the ceremony, which Irwin and Rubenstein witnessed, they left the registry office and started their honeymoon.

Vaughan hired a cottage in a lonely part of the country and here, for the following two weeks, they forgot about bats and spaceships and were happy. They rambled about the countryside and swam in the river, or fished from a boat that had been lent them; led a carefree existence that was but the preamble to their future life together. It was the first time they had been really alone, and they discovered a new contentment in each other's company.

The days sped by, the honeymoon ended, and they returned to headquarters.

Dobson was back, and he had news for them.

'I've got something, I think. An amplifying-and-broadcasting unit of sufficient power to make a test sortie! It didn't happen as easily as that, however — you can't imagine the snags we've had to iron out. I don't suppose I've had more than a

few hours sleep in the last two weeks — '
He looked exhausted, his skin pale, and there were dark rings about his eyes. ' — but we've done it!'

Irwin put them in the picture, and Vaughan and Ann began to realize how fast the scientists had worked in their absence.

'We've set up research units in fifty different places; on remote islands, in the jungles of South America, in Siberia, Tibet, and in the Arctic; in caves and on mountains. I'm prepared to swear that the bats can't get at every experimental group without blasting the planet apart! If this thing works, we're set to go ahead in a big way.'

Vaughan asked: 'And the enemy? They're doing nothing about it?'

Irwin shrugged.

'They're ignoring us, as usual. They still maintain watch over the world's capitals, and their ships land to pick up new batches of metal. There's just no way of telling how much they know.'

Vaughan frowned.

'I don't like it,' he said.

'Well, we'll know tomorrow . . . '

Tomorrow dawned . . . the day of the test. Dobson's equipment was already in place and one of his assistants had volunteered to wear the new helmet.

The place was Cornwall. The metal tin. The time noon.

Vaughan went down as observer and watched from a distance through powerful binoculars. An old shed served as headquarters for the scientists; here, their equipment sprawled in a labyrinth of gadgets and wiring. A stand-by generator set was running in case the main supply failed.

Workmen brought out the tin and stacked it on open ground, then retired. They waited for the bats to come.

Dobson consulted his watch.

'Five minutes yet.'

His assistant was already sitting in a chair, helmet in place. Dobson's hand rested on the main switch, ready to throw power into his circuits and spring the thought-web. The sky was clear.

Three minutes . . .

A grey, ovoid shape appeared in the

sky, high up, grew larger. Down swooped the spaceship, down towards the stack of tin on the ground.

Vaughan watched through his glasses. He saw the ship land and the bats fly out. They assembled in a circle about the metal . . . and, slowly, it began to disappear.

Dobson's hand jerked down the switch-handle. Power surged through the cables; thought was amplified, broadcast . . . the whole area was filled with thought-waves, invisible to the eye, but still incredibly powerful.

Vaughan sweated, his hands shaking. Something must happen soon. The bats could not be unaware of this interference . . . surely their telepathic powers must falter?

Nothing happened. The invaders did not move and the tinplate continued to vanish before Vaughan's eyes, teleported into the spaceship. Not until the last piece of metal had disappeared did the invaders return to their ship. The circular port closed and the spaceship rose, gathering speed. In another two minutes

270

it was out of sight.

Vaughan lowered his glasses, bitterness welling up inside. Dobson's weapon had failed. The aliens had not even noticed anything unusual — or if they had, refused to bother with it. Their mental powers were so far in excess of anything Earth could produce that they completely ignored the attack.

18

Thought Barrier

There was an official enquiry, of course. Dobson double-checked his apparatus and stated, definitely, that the area had been saturated with thought-waves. The final conclusion could only be that human thought-waves had no disturbing effect on the bats . . .

It was a shattering blow. Earth was once more hopeless before the invaders. Their spaceships hung in the sky and fresh demands for metals were made. Research still went on, but the heart had gone out of the scientists. They tried to develop a more powerful screen, and experimented with a distortion effect, superimposing the waves one on another. There were more tests — and more failures. The bats ignored everything.

Only Vaughan continued to believe in the new weapon.

'I'm sure we're on the right track,' he said to Ann, 'it's just that we haven't discovered the right approach. We will . . . it's only a question of time. We've got to keep at it. Maybe we should vary the wave-length — '

'What's the use?' Ann wanted to know. 'If this weapon were really dangerous, they'd teleport more hydrogen bombs and stop our research.'

'Not necessarily. In fact, simply because they ignore us makes me hopeful. They must realize by now we've so many research units operating that they could only hope to stop us by destroying the whole Earth — and they need metals too badly to do that. So they're keeping quiet and hoping we'll drop the ideas as a failure. That's how I see it.'

'You may be right,' Ann replied carelessly.

She had changed since their marriage, Vaughan realized. Right away, she had resigned from the American Intelligence Service; but it wasn't only that. She had lost interest in world affairs, almost as if she accepted the domination of the Earth by bats as something natural. Her life centred around making a home for the family they planned, and she had no time for anything else.

Irwin was plunged in gloom; he thought Dobson's new experiments a waste of time and saw no hope in ever defeating the invaders. The Prime Minister, too, only sanctioned the research because no one offered an alternative plan. It was a time of waiting . . .

A month passed, and Earth's resources continued to be shipped to the moon, then to the unknown home of the bat-people among the stars. Dobson paid the Vaughans a visit.

They sat on the lawn of Vaughan's riverside bungalow, overlooking the lower reaches of the Thames. A blue sky was mirrored in the smoothly flowing water. In the distance, a white triangle of sail showed through the trees and a line of ducks went swimming past.

'I've about come to the end of my ideas,' Dobson confessed sombrely. 'I've tried all the variations I can think of — experimented with the brain impulses of all manner of people, from labourers to dons and poets to machinists. I'm stuck! I can't see my way clear — '

Vaughan started in his chair, an idea forming in his head. The quality of the brain to be broadcast was something he had not considered. He felt a sudden surge of excitement.

'Tell me about the people you've used,' he demanded.

Dobson said: 'Well, all sorts. To start with, I used anyone to hand; then I thought it might be important and became selective. I tried the creative mind several times; a painter, a musician, a poet. Then I switched to routine workers; then to — '

Ann interrupted: 'I think I see what Neil is driving at. He means that we must find an opposite kind of mind to that of the moon raiders.'

Vaughan concentrated. Some new idea formed in his head, but refused to take on words. He felt frustrated.

'Opposite to what?' Dobson wanted to know. 'So far, the bats have shown themselves to be completely logical, governed entirely by their instinctive urge for survival. In that respect, every human being is identical.'

'Not everyone!' The idea clicked in Vaughan's brain and he came out of his chair as if catapulted. 'Not everyone,' he repeated triumphantly.

Dobson and Ann looked at him, waiting for him to explain. Vaughan spoke one word, softly:

'*Insanity!*'

Dobson's breath hissed.

'Yes, that might work . . . the thought impulses of the insane . . . broadcast a network of thought-waves from would-be suicides . . . the urge to self-destruction. We can use manic-depressive types, or schizophrenics . . . that should give the invaders something to worry about!'

Ann nodded to herself.

'I think you've got it, Neil. A world-wide broadcast of thought-waves from patients in mental homes.'

'It might be dangerous to test this idea,' Vaughan said thoughtfully. 'If we are on the right track, a limited screen could be fatal — the aliens would still be free to teleport hydrogen bombs anywhere else on Earth. We've got to go all out this time.'

Dobson got to his feet.

'I'm going to contact the government right away,' he said, and hurried off.

After he had gone, Ann moved close to her husband and slipped her arm through his. They both looked up at the sky, seeing beyond to the infinity of space.

Ann whispered: 'Free again to control our destiny — is it possible?'

Vaughan put his arms round her and kissed her gently.

'It's possible,' he said.

The government acted swiftly. America and Russia were informed of the new plan and scientists all over the world went to work.

Dobson's apparatus was mass-produced, the co-operation of hospital authorities and individuals and their families, obtained. Where there were objections on the grounds of human rights violation they were ruthlessly ignored: this was a global emergency. At last, the hook-up was ready . . .

Vaughan stood in a secret operations room with Irwin and the Prime Minister. A clock on the wall pointed the time: 15.55 hours.

Irwin said: 'In five minutes from now, the moon raiders are due to pick up a consignment of metal. An observer on the spot will phone through immediately they start to teleport — and we give the signal to raise the thought-barrier. This time we must win!'

The Premier did not speak. Vaughan tried to imagine Dobson's men connecting their apparatus, the white-coated medical orderlies, the patients strapped to chairs and helmeted, ready. More than one thousand mentally deranged persons had been 'persuaded' to take part in the experiment; and scientists had now achieved amplification to the order of five thousand times. Where anyone resisted, force was used. So far as the scientists were concerned, the more mental turmoil the patients were experiencing the better. It was inhuman, ruthless — but necessary. In effect, a barrage of five million irrational minds was about to be flung at the invaders.

Vaughan wondered just how sensitive the bats' telepathic brains were — and what would happen to them.

'Three minutes,' Irwin said.

They looked at each other, remembering a similar waiting period. The moon rocket had been destroyed; this time, the bats must destroy the world if they were to prevent the attack. It was an anxious moment . . .

'One minute.'

Vaughan thought about his wife, and wished he were with her instead of here in this underground hideout. If the enemy did launch hydrogen bombs . . . he blocked out the thought.

The seconds hand of the dock was creeping round to zero hour. A phone rang. Irwin took it.

'Yes . . . I hear you . . . keep us informed . . . I'll keep the line open.'

He turned and said: 'A spaceship is landing to pick up the metal. We'll know the worst very soon now.'

The hands of the clock passed the hour mark.

Irwin listened to his observer, repeating his remarks: 'The bats have landed and are now in a circle about the metal.'

The Prime Minister's hand rested on the button that would transmit a signal round the world.

Irwin said, calmly: 'They have started to teleport.'

Vaughan took a deep breath. In the next few seconds . . . The Prime Minister pressed the button . . . tiny electrical impulses went out from the operations room and tripped mechanisms in a thousand different places. On the instant, Dobson's machines operated automatically.

There was nothing to see. An invisible network of thought-waves covered the Earth; from Europe and Asia, from America and Africa, from islands and the Antarctic ice, thought-impulses of the insane formed a barrier about the world. Vaughan tried to imagine what effect it would have on the creatures from the moon . . . the equivalent of five million unbalanced minds broadcasting at once.

If it had any effect on them at all,

the result could only be shattering. The bats' logical thought-processes would be swamped by waves of thought deprived of all rational content; suicides driven by an urge to self-destruction; split minds; the awful melancholy of the depressed; frustrations and inhibitions; an unlocking of secret corners of the mind, confusion and chaos . . .

Irwin, still holding the phone, said: '*They have stopped teleporting!*'

Vaughan felt a tremendous weight slip from him. They had won!

The thought-broadcast continued. Insanity, unleashed and amplified, beat in relentless waves upon the bat-people destroying their capacity to teleport or communicate telepathically with each other. Each of them was now isolated, cut off from their race mind. They were animals, defenceless, helpless . . .

'They are retreating to the ship,' Irwin reported. 'The bulk of the metal is still outside the ship. Their movements lack co-ordination and they are behaving like any other horde of frightened creatures.'

Yes, Vaughan thought, that would be

the bat-people's dominant emotion — fear! Never before could they have experienced anything like this. Perhaps they do not understand what has happened, but simply panicked under the stream of senseless thought that has assailed their minds.

'Cars mounting machine-guns are attacking the bats,' Irwin said from the phone. 'Several have been killed. They have no defence against us now.'

Vaughan felt sickened. This was slaughter, not war. He remembered Paris . . . the invaders must be taught a lesson: Earth must be left alone.

'Another spaceship is coming down. It is . . . no, it's out of control. It's crashing! There's — '

Irwin stopped speaking. He rattled the bar of the handset.

'Line's dead,' he explained briefly.

Vaughan switched on the radio transmitter and spoke into the microphone.

'Operations room. Any observers at point X report on the position immediately.'

Back came the reply: 'Enemy ship

crashed and atomic engine exploded. No sign of life from the area.'

Vaughan heaved a sigh of relief. For a moment, he thought the bats had, in some way, nullified their thought-barrier. He guessed the truth, and turned to the Premier.

'Their ships are run by automatic devices, controlled by thought-waves. Our screen has destroyed that control — I expect there'll be more crashes.'

They listened to radio reports that came in from all parts of the world. One ship down over New York, another in Russia; one in the Channel — the explosion caused a tidal wave that sent the sea churning up the Thames, flooding a vast area.

There was a great silence.

Vaughan said grimly: 'We can be sure that no bat lives on our world, that no spaceship rides our sky. The rest depends on what action the bat-people at the moon base take . . . we can only wait.'

The Prime Minister got a direct telephone line to Greenwich observatory.

'Watch the moon,' he said.

Minutes passed, and Greenwich reported: 'A ship has appeared from behind the moon, heading for Earth.'

More waiting, hours this time. Had the bats a weapon to beat the thought-barrier? Vaughan phoned Ann and told her the news.

How far out into space would the screen be operative? Routine checks came regularly from Greenwich. The ship was entering Earth's atmosphere. It came down, down . . .

From the radio an excited voice acclaimed: 'It's crashed! They have no defence against the thought-barrier. We've won!'

The Prime Minister was smiling, Irwin looked stunned. There was still the base on the other side of the moon, but now Earth could build a ship and send a hydrogen bomb to destroy it. The thought-barrier made that possible . . .

Greenwich came through again. The Prime Minister took the call; when he replaced the receiver, there were tears in his eyes.

'It's over,' he said. 'A fleet of ships has

been observed leaving the moon — not for Earth, but *away from the solar system*. I don't think they'll be coming back.'

Vaughan went up into the sunlight. He stood a while looking at the countryside, breathing the scent of flowers, listening to the song of the birds. The sky was blue and dotted with puffs of white cloud and he was very happy.

Earth belonged to men once more. The threat of alien domination from another planet no longer hung in the sky like the sword of Damocles. The Earth and its civilization had been violated. Much of Western Europe was still in turmoil after the Paris bombing. It would take time to replace the lost metals, and even longer for the harmful radioactivity to die down. A long time to put the world to rights again, but it could — and would — be done. A united world, this time . . .

He turned away, whistling, a new springiness in his stride. He started his car and drove home.

We do hope that you have enjoyed reading this large print book.

Did you know that all of our titles are available for purchase?

We publish a wide range of high quality large print books including:
Romances, Mysteries, Classics
General Fiction
Non Fiction and Westerns

Special interest titles available in large print are:
The Little Oxford Dictionary
Music Book, Song Book
Hymn Book, Service Book

Also available from us courtesy of Oxford University Press:
Young Readers' Dictionary
(large print edition)
Young Readers' Thesaurus
(large print edition)

For further information or a free brochure, please contact us at:
Ulverscroft Large Print Books Ltd.,
The Green, Bradgate Road, Anstey,
Leicester, LE7 7FU, England.
Tel: (00 44) **0116 236 4325**
Fax: (00 44) **0116 234 0205**

SCORPION: SECOND GENERATION

Michael R. Linaker

The colony of deadly scorpions at Long Point Nuclear Plant was eradicated. Or so people thought . . . Over a year later, entomologist Miles Ranleigh receives a worrying telephone call. A man has been fatally poisoned by toxic venom, identical to the Long Point scorpions' — but far more powerful. Miles and his companion Jill Ansty must race to destroy the fresh infestation. But this is a new strain of scorpion. Mutated and irradiated, they're larger, more savage — and infected with a deadly virus fatal to humans. And they're breeding . . .

THE RITTER DOUBLE CROSS

Frederick Nolan

In Nazi Germany, in 1941, there was a factory in the north German town of Seelze. Though officially its function was a top military secret, it was known to be associated with the manufacture of poison gases. Until a raid put the factory out of action ... Based on fact, this is the story of five men who were parachuted in to Seelze to destroy the chemical plant. But the Gestapo were waiting — and one of the five was a traitor ...

THE TRAVELS OF SHERLOCK HOLMES

John Hall

Secrecy surrounds the supposed death of Sherlock Holmes in 1891 — and his re-emergence three years later. What happened to him during the missing years of his life? This story of those missing years reveals how Holmes foiled his old adversary and became involved in a terrible game; its prize, the mastery of an entire continent — India. Holmes' adventures take him to Tibet, Persia and the Sudan, but as sole representative of the British Government, his life and the British Empire is at stake.